AF624990

CASSELL'S NATIONAL LIBRARY

THE CASTLE OF OTRANTO

CASSELL'S NATIONAL LIBRARY

THE CASTLE OF OTRANTO

BY

HORACE WALPOLE

KALPAZ

©Reserved

All rights reserved. No part of this work may be reproduced, stored, adapted, or transmitted in any form or by any means, electronic, mechanical, photocopying, micro-filming recording or otherwise, or translated in any language, without the prior written permission of the copyright owner and the publisher. The book is sold subject to the condition that it shall not, by way of trade or otherwise, be lent, resold, hired out, or otherwise circulated without the prior publisher's written consent in any form of binding or cover other than that in which it is published.

The views and opinions expressed in this book are author(s) own and the facts reported by them have been verified to the extent possible, and the publishers are not in any way liable for the same.

ISBN: 978-93-5128-364-5(PB)

First Published in 1886
Indian Reprint in 2017

Published by

Kalpaz Publications
C-30, Satyawati Nagar,
Delhi – 110052
E-mail: kalpaz@hotmail.com
Website: kalpazpublications.com
Ph.: +91-9212142040

Cataloging in Publication Data—DK

Courtesy: D.K. Agencies (P) Ltd. <docinfo@dkagencies.com>

Walpole, Horace, 1717-1797, **author.**

The castle of Otranto / by Horace Walpole.
pages cm
Novel.
"First published in 1886"
ISBN 9789351283645 (PB)

1. Inheritance and succession—Fiction. 2. Castles—Fiction. 3. Italy—Fiction. 4. Gothic fiction (Literary genre), English. I. Title.

PR3757.W2C37 2017 DDC 823.6 23

INTRODUCTION

Horace Walpole was the youngest son of Sir Robert Walpole, the greatstatesman, who died Earl of Orford. He was born in 1717, the year inwhich his father resigned office, remaining in opposition for almostthree years before his return to a long tenure of power. Horace Walpolewas educated at Eton, where he formed a school friendship with Thomas Gray, who was but a few months older. In 1739 Gray wastravelling-companion with Walpole in France and Italy until they differedand parted; but the friendship was afterwards renewed, and remained firmto the end. Horace Walpole went from Eton to King's College, Cambridge,and entered Parliament in 1741, the year before his father's finalresignation and acceptance of an earldom. His way of life was made easyto him. As Usher of the Exchequer, Comptroller of the Pipe, and Clerk ofthe Estreats in the Exchequer, he received nearly two thousand a year fordoing nothing, lived with his father, and amused himself.

Horace Walpole idled, and amused himself with the small life of thefashionable world to which he was proud of belonging, though he had aquick eye for its vanities. He had social wit, and liked to put it tosmall uses. But he was not an empty idler, and there were seasons whenhe could become a sharp judge of himself. "I am sensible," he wrote tohis most intimate friend, "I am sensible of having more follies andweaknesses and fewer real good qualities than most men. I sometimesreflect on this, though, I own, too seldom. I always want to beginacting like a man, and a sensible one, which I think I might be if Iwould." He had deep home affections, and, under many politeaffectations, plenty of good sense.Horace Walpole's father died in 1745. The eldest son, who succeeded tothe earldom, died in 1751, and left a son, George, who was for a timeinsane, and lived until 1791.

As George left no child, the title andestates passed to Horace Walpole, then seventy-four years old, and theonly uncle who survived. Horace Walpole thus became Earl of Orford,during the last six years of his life. As to the title, he said that hefelt himself being called names in his old age. He died unmarried, inthe year 1797, at the age of eighty.

He had turned his house at Strawberry Hill, by the Thames, near Twickenham, into a Gothic villa—eighteenth-century Gothic—and amusedhimself by spending freely upon its adornment with such things as werethen fashionable as objects of taste. But he delighted also in hisflowers and his trellises of roses, and the quiet Thames. When confinedby gout to his London house in Arlington Street, flowers from Strawberry Hill and a bird were necessary consolations. He set up also at Strawberry Hill a private printing press, at which he printed his friend Gray's poems, also in 1758 his own "Catalogue of the Royal and Noble Authors of England," and five volumes of "Anecdotes of Painting in England," between 1762 and 1771.

Horace Walpole produced _The Castle of Otranto_ in 1765, at the matureage of forty-eight. It was suggested by a dream from which he said hewaked one morning, and of which "all I could recover was, that I hadthought myself in an ancient castle (a very natural dream for a head likemine, filled with Gothic story), and that on the uppermost banister of agreat staircase I saw a gigantic hand in armour. In the evening I satdown and began to write, without knowing in the least what I intended tosay or relate." So began the tale which professed to be translated by "William Marshal, gentleman, from the Italian of Onuphro Muralto, canonof the Church of St. Nicholas, at Otranto." It was written in twomonths. Walpole's friend Gray reported to him that at Cambridge the bookmade "some of them cry a little, and all in general afraid to go to bedo' nights." _The Castle of Otranto_ was, in its own way, an early signof the reaction towards romance in the latter part of the last century. This gives it interest. But it has had many followers, and the hardymodern reader, when he read's Gray's note from Cambridge, needs to bereminded of its date.

PREFACE

TO THE FIRST EDITION.

The following work was found in the library of an ancient Catholicfamily in the north of England. It was printed at Naples, in theblack letter, in the year 1529. How much sooner it was written doesnot appear. The principal incidents are such as were believed in thedarkest ages of Christianity; but the language and conduct havenothing that savours of barbarism. The style is the purest Italian.

If the story was written near the time when it is supposed to havehappened, it must have been between 1095, the era of the first Crusade, and 1243, the date of the last, or not long afterwards. There is no other circumstance in the work that can lead us to guessat the period in which the scene is laid: the names of the actors areevidently fictitious, and probably disguised on purpose: yet the Spanish names of the domestics seem to indicate that this work was notcomposed until the establishment of the Arragonian Kings in Naples hadmade Spanish appellations familiar in that country. The beauty of thediction, and the zeal of the author (moderated, however, by singularjudgment) concur to make me think that the date of the composition waslittle antecedent to that of the impression. Letters were then intheir most flourishing state in Italy, and contributed to dispel theempire of superstition, at that time so forcibly attacked by thereformers. It is not unlikely that an artful priest might endeavourto turn their own arms on the innovators, and might avail himself ofhis abilities as an author to confirm the populace in their ancienterrors and superstitions. If this was his view, he has certainlyacted withsig naladdress.Such a work as the following would enslavea hundred vulgar minds beyond half the books of controversy that havebeen written from the days of Luther to the present hour.

This solution of the author's motives is, however, offered as a mereconjecture. Whatever his views were, or whatever effects theexecution of them might have, his work can only be laid before thepublic at present as a matter of entertainment. Even as such, someapology for it is necessary. Miracles, visions, necromancy, dreams,and other preternatural events, are exploded now even from romances. That was not the case when our author wrote; much less when the storyitself is supposed to have happened. Belief in every kind of prodigywas so established in those dark ages, that an author would not befaithful to the manners of the times, who should omit all mention ofthem. He is not bound to believe them himself, but he must representhis actors as believing them.

If this air of the miraculous is excused, the reader will find nothingelse unworthy of his perusal. Allow the possibility of the facts, andall the actors comport themselves as persons would do in theirsituation. There is no bombast, no similes, flowers, digressions, orunnecessary descriptions. Everything tends directly to thecatastrophe. Never is the reader's attention relaxed. The rules ofthe drama are almost observed throughout the conduct of the piece. The characters are well drawn, and still better maintained. Terror,the author's principal engine, prevents the story from everlanguishing; and it is so often contrasted by pity, that the mind iskept up in a constant vicissitude of interesting passions.

Some persons may perhaps think the characters of the domestics toolittle serious for the general cast of the story; but besides theiropposition to the principal personages, the art of the author is veryobservable in his conduct of the subalterns. They discover manypassages essential to the story, which could not be well brought tolight but by their NAIVETE and simplicity. In particular, thewomanish terror and foibles of Bianca, in the last chapter, conduceessentially towards advancing the catastrophe.

It is natural for a translator to be prejudiced in favour of hisadopted work. More impartial readers may not be so much struck withthe beauties of this piece as I was. Yet I am not blind to myauthor's defects.

I could wish he had grounded his plan on a moreuseful moral than this: that "the sins of fathers are visited ontheir children to the third and fourth generation." I doubt whether,in his time, any more than at present, ambition curbed its appetite ofdominion from the dread of so remote a punishment. And yet this moralis weakened by that less direct insinuation, that even such anathemamay be diverted by devotion to St. Nicholas. Here the interest of the Monk plainly gets the better of the judgment of the author. However,with all its faults, I have no doubt but the English reader will bepleased with a sight of this performance. The piety that reignsthroughout, the lessons of virtue that are inculcated, and the rigidpurity of the sentiments, exempt this work from the censure to whichromances are but too liable. Should it meet with the success I hopefor, I may be encouraged to reprint the original Italian, though itwill tend to depreciate my own labour. Our language falls far shortof the charms of the Italian, both for variety and harmony. Thelatter is peculiarly excellent for simple narrative. It is difficultin English to relate without falling too low or rising too high; afault obviously occasioned by the little care taken to speak purelanguage in common conversation. Every Italian or Frenchman of anyrank piques himself on speaking his own tongue correctly and withchoice. I cannot flatter myself with having done justice to my authorin this respect: his style is as elegant as his conduct of thepassions is masterly. It is a pity that he did not apply his talentsto what they were evidently proper for - the theatre.

I will detain the reader no longer, but to make one short remark. Though the machinery is invention, and the names of the actorsimaginary, I cannot but believe that the groundwork of the story isfounded on truth. The scene is undoubtedly laid in some real castle. The author seems frequently, without design, to describe particularparts. "The chamber," says he, "on the right hand;" "the door on theleft hand;" "the distance from the chapel to Conrad's apartment:"these and other passages are strong presumptions that the author hadsome certain building in his eye. Curious persons, who have leisureto employ in such researches, may possibly discover in the Italianwriters the foundation on which our author has built. If acatastrophe, at all resembling that which he describes, is believed tohave given rise to this work, it will contribute to interest thereader, and will make the "Castle of Otranto a still more movingstory.

SONNET

TO

THE RIGHT HONOURABLE LADY MARY COKE.

The gentle maid, whose hapless tale
These melancholy pages speak;
Say, gracious lady, shall she fail
To draw the tear adown thy cheek?
No; never was thy pitying breast
Insensible to human woes;
Tender, tho' firm, it melts distrest
For weaknesses it never knows.
Oh! guard the marvels I relate
Of fell ambition scourg'd by fate,
From reason's peevish blame.
Blest with thy smile, my dauntless sail
I dare expand to Fancy's gale,
For sure thy smiles are Fame.

H. W.

CHAPTER - I

MANFRED, Prince of Otranto, had one son and one daughter: the latter,a most beautiful virgin, aged eighteen, was called Matilda. Conrad,the son, was three years younger, a homely youth, sickly, and of nopromising disposition; yet he was the darling of his father, who nevershowed any symptoms of affection to Matilda. Manfred had contracted amarriage for his son with the Marquis of Vicenza's daughter, Isabella;and she had already been delivered by her guardians into the hands of Manfred, that he might celebrate the wedding as soon as Conrad'sinfirm state of health would permit.

Manfred's impatience for this ceremonial was remarked by his familyand neighbours. The former, indeed, apprehending the severity oftheir Prince's disposition, did not dare to utter their surmises onthis precipitation. Hippolita, his wife, an amiable lady, didsometimes venture to represent the danger of marrying their only sonso early, considering his great youth, and greater infirmities; butshe never received any other answer than reflections on her ownsterility, who had given him but one heir. His tenants and subjectswere less cautious in their discourses. They attributed this hastywedding to the Prince's dread of seeing accomplished an ancientprophecy, which was said to have pronounced that the castle andlordship of Otranto "should pass from the present family, whenever thereal owner should be grown too large to inhabit it." It was difficultto make any sense of this prophecy; and still less easy to conceivewhat it had to do with the marriage in question. Yet these mysteries,or contradictions, did not make the populace adhere the less to theiropinion.

Young Conrad's birthday was fixed for his espousals. The company wasassembled in the chapel of the Castle, and everything ready forbeginning the divine office, when Conrad himself was missing.

Manfred, impatient of the least delay, and who had not observed hisson retire, despatched one of his attendants to summon the young Prince. The servant, who had not stayed long enough to have crossedthe court to Conrad's apartment, came running back breathless, in afrantic manner, his eyes staring, and foaming at the month. He saidnothing, but pointed to the court.

The company were struck with terror and amazement. The Princess Hippolita, without knowing what was the matter, but anxious for herson, swooned away. Manfred, less apprehensive than enraged at theprocrastination of the nuptials, and at the folly of his domestic,asked imperiously what was the matter? The fellow made no answer, butcontinued pointing towards the court-yard; and at last, after repeatedquestions put to him, cried out, "Oh! the helmet! the helmet!"

In the meantime, some of the company had run into the court, fromwhence was heard a confused noise of shrieks, horror, and surprise.

Manfred, who began to be alarmed at not seeing his son, went himselfto get information of what occasioned this strange confusion. Matildaremained endeavouring to assist her mother, and Isabella stayed forthe same purpose, and to avoid showing any impatience for thebridegroom, for whom, in truth, she had conceived little affection.

The first thing that struck Manfred's eyes was a group of his servantsendeavouring to raise something that appeared to him a mountain ofsable plumes. He gazed without believing his sight.

"What are ye doing?" cried Manfred, wrathfully; "where is my son?"

A volley of voices replied, "Oh! my Lord! the Prince! the Prince! thehelmet! the helmet!"

Shocked with these lamentable sounds, and dreading he knew not what,he advanced hastily, - but what a sight for a father's eyes! - hebeheld his child dashed to pieces, and almost buried under an enormoushelmet, an hundred times more large than any casque ever made forhuman being, and shaded with a proportionable quantity of blackfeathers.

The horror of the spectacle, the ignorance of all around how thismisfortune had happened, and above all, the tremendous phenomenonbefore him, took away the Prince's speech. Yet his silence lastedlonger than even grief could occasion. He fixed his eyes on what hewished in vain to believe a vision; and seemed less attentive to hisloss, than buried in meditation on the stupendous object that hadoccasioned it. He touched, he examined the fatal casque; nor couldeven the bleeding mangled remains of the young Prince divert the eyesof Manfred from the portent before him.

All who had known his partial fondness for young Conrad, were as muchsurprised at their Prince's insensibility, as thunderstruck themselvesat the miracle of the helmet. They conveyed the disfigured corpseinto the hall, without receiving the least direction from Manfred. Aslittle was he attentive to the ladies who remained in the chapel. Onthe contrary, without mentioning the unhappy princesses, his wife anddaughter, the first sounds that dropped from Manfred's lips were, "Take care of the Lady Isabella."

The domestics, without observing the singularity of this direction,were guided by their affection to their mistress, to consider it aspeculiarly addressed to her situation, and flew to her assistance. They conveyed her to her chamber more dead than alive, and indifferentto all the strange circumstances she heard, except the death of herson.

Matilda, who doted on her mother, smothered her own grief andamazement, and thought of nothing but assisting and comforting herafflicted parent. Isabella, who had been treated by Hippolita like adaughter, and who returned that tenderness with equal duty andaffection, was scarce less assiduous about the Princess; at the sametime endeavouring to partake and lessen the weight of sorrow which shesaw Matilda strove to suppress, for whom she had conceived the warmestsympathy of friendship. Yet her own situation could not help findingits place in her thoughts. She felt no concern for the death of young Conrad, except commiseration; and she was not sorry to be deliveredfrom a marriage which had promised her little felicity, either fromher destined bridegroom, or from the severe temper of Manfred, who,though he had distinguished her by great indulgence, had imprinted hermind with terror, from his causeless rigour to such amiable princessesesas Hippolita and Matilda.

While the ladies were conveying the wretched mother to her bed, Manfred remained in the court, gazing on the ominous casque, andregardless of the crowd which the strangeness of the event had nowassembled around him. The few words he articulated, tended solely toinquiries, whether any man knew from whence it could have come? Nobody could give him the least information. However, as it seemed tobe the sole object of his curiosity, it soon became so to the rest ofthe spectators, whose conjectures were as absurd and improbable, asthe catastrophe itself was unprecedented. In the midst of theirsenseless guesses, a young peasant, whom rumour had drawn thither froma neighbouring village, observed that the miraculous helmet wasexactly like that on the figure in black marble of Alfonso the Good,one of their former princes, in the church of St. Nicholas.

"Villain! What sayest thou?" cried Manfred, starting from his trancein a tempest of rage, and seizing the young man by the collar; "howdarest thou utter such treason? Thy life shall pay for it."

The spectators, who as little comprehended the cause of the Prince'sfury as all the rest they had seen, were at a loss to unravel this newcircumstance. The young peasant himself was still more astonished,not conceiving how he had offended the Prince. Yet recollectinghimself, with a mixture of grace and humility, he disengaged himselffrom Manfred's grip, and then with an obeisance, which discovered morejealousy of innocence than dismay, he asked, with respect, of what hewas guilty? Manfred, more enraged at the vigour, however decentlyexerted, with which the young man had shaken off his hold, thanappeased by his submission, ordered his attendants to seize him, and,if he had not been withheld by his friends whom he had invited to thenuptials, would have poignarded the peasant in their arms.

During this altercation, some of the vulgar spectators had run to thegreat church, which stood near the castle, and came back open-mouthed,declaring that the helmet was missing from Alfonso's statue. Manfred,at this news, grew perfectly frantic; and, as if he sought a subjecton which to vent the tempest within him, he rushed again on the youngpeasant, crying -

"Villain! Monster! Sorcerer! 'tis thou hast done this! 'tis thou hastslain my son!"

The mob, who wanted some object within the scope of their capacities,on whom they might discharge their bewildered reasoning, caught thewords from the mouth of their lord, and re-echoed -

"Ay, ay; 'tis he, 'tis he: he has stolen the helmet from good Alfonso's tomb, and dashed out the brains of our young Prince withit," never reflecting how enormous the disproportion was between themarble helmet that had been in the church, and that of steel beforetheir eyes; nor how impossible it was for a youth seemingly nottwenty, to wield a piece of armour of so prodigious a weight

The folly of these ejaculations brought Manfred to himself: yetwhether provoked at the peasant having observed the resemblancebetween the two helmets, and thereby led to the farther discovery ofthe absence of that in the church, or wishing to bury any such rumourunder so impertinent a supposition, he gravely pronounced that theyoung man was certainly a necromancer, and that till the Church couldtake cognisance of the affair, he would have the Magician, whom theyhad thus detected, kept prisoner under the helmet itself, which heordered his attendants to raise, and place the young man under it;declaring he should be kept there without food, with which his owninfernal art might furnish him.

It was in vain for the youth to represent against this preposteroussentence: in vain did Manfred's friends endeavour to divert him fromthis savage and ill-grounded resolution. The generality were charmedwith their lord's decision, which, to their apprehensions, carriedgreat appearance of justice, as the Magician was to be punished by thevery instrument with which he had offended: nor were they struck withthe least compunction at the probability of the youth being starved,for they firmly believed that, by his diabolic skill, he could easilysupply himself with nutriment.

Manfred thus saw his commands even cheerfully obeyed; and appointing aguard with strict orders to prevent any food being conveyed to theprisoner, he dismissed his friends and attendants, and retired to hisown chamber, after locking the gates of the castle, in which hesuffered none but his domestics to remain.

In the meantime, the care and zeal of the young Ladies had brought the Princess Hippolita to herself, who amidst the transports of her ownsorrow frequently demanded news of her lord, would have dismissed herattendants to watch over him, and at last enjoined Matilda to leaveher, and visit and comfort her father. Matilda, who wanted noaffectionate duty to Manfred, though she trembled at his austerity,obeyed the orders of Hippolita, whom she tenderly recommended to Isabella; and inquiring of the domestics for her father, was informedthat he was retired to his chamber, and had commanded that nobodyshould have admittance to him. Concluding that he was immersed insorrow for the death of her brother, and fearing to renew his tears bythe sight of his sole remaining child, she hesitated whether sheshould break in upon his affliction; yet solicitude for him, backed bythe commands of her mother, encouraged her to venture disobeying theorders he had given; a fault she had never been guilty of before.

The gentle timidity of her nature made her pause for some minutes athis door. She heard him traverse his chamber backwards, and forwardswith disordered steps; a mood which increased her apprehensions. Shewas, however, just going to beg admittance, when Manfred suddenlyopened the door; and as it was now twilight, concurring with thedisorder of his mind, he did not distinguish the person, but askedangrily, who it was? Matilda replied, trembling -

"My dearest father, it is I, your daughter."

Manfred, stepping back hastily, cried, "Begone! I do not want adaughter;" and flinging back abruptly, clapped the door against theterrified Matilda.

She was too well acquainted with her father's impetuosity to venture asecond intrusion. When she had a little recovered the shock of sobitter a reception, she wiped away her tears to prevent the additionalstab that the knowledge of it would give to Hippolita, who questionedher in the most anxious terms on the health of Manfred, and how hebore his loss. Matilda assured her he was well, and supported hismisfortune with manly fortitude.

"But will he not let me see him?" said Hippolita mournfully; "will henot permit me to blend my tears with his, and shed a mother's sorrowsin the bosom of her Lord? Or do you deceive me, Matilda? I know how Manfred doted on his son: is not the stroke too heavy for him? has henot sunk under it? You do not answer me - alas! I dread the worst! -Raise me, my maidens; I will, I will see my Lord. Bear me to himinstantly: he is dearer to me even than my children."

Matilda made signs to Isabella to prevent Hippolita's rising; and boththose lovely young women were using their gentle violence to stop andcalm the Princess, when a servant, on the part of Manfred, arrived andtold Isabella that his Lord demanded to speak with her.

"With me!" cried Isabella.

"Go," said Hippolita, relieved by a message from her Lord: "Manfredcannot support the sight of his own family. He thinks you lessdisordered than we are, and dreads the shock of my grief. Consolehim, dear Isabella, and tell him I will smother my own anguish ratherthan add to his."

As it was now evening the servant who conducted Isabella bore a torchbefore her. When they came to Manfred, who was walking impatientlyabout the gallery, he started, and said hastily -

"Take away that light, and begone."

Then shutting the door impetuously, he flung himself upon a benchagainst the wall, and bade Isabella sit by him. She obeyed trembling.

"I sent for you, Lady," said he - and then stopped under greatappearance of confusion.

"My Lord!"

"Yes, I sent for you on a matter of great moment," resumed he. "Dryyour tears, young Lady - you have lost your bridegroom. Yes, cruelfate! and I have lost the hopes of my race! But Conrad was not worthyof your beauty."

"How, my Lord!" said Isabella; "sure you do not suspect me of notfeeling the concern I ought: my duty and affection would have always

"Think no more of him," interrupted Manfred; "he was a sickly, punychild, and Heaven has perhaps taken him away, that I might not trustthe honours of my house on so frail a foundation. The line of Manfredcalls for numerous supports. My foolish fondness for that boy blindedthe eyes of my prudence - but it is better as it is. I hope, in a fewyears, to have reason to rejoice at the death of Conrad."

Words cannot paint the astonishment of Isabella. At first sheapprehended that grief had disordered Manfred's understanding. Hernext thought suggested that this strange discourse was designed toensnare her: she feared that Manfred had perceived her indifferencefor his son: and in consequence of that idea she replied -

"Good my Lord, do not doubt my tenderness: my heart would haveaccompanied my hand. Conrad would have engrossed all my care; andwherever fate shall dispose of me, I shall always cherish his memory,and regard your Highness and the virtuous Hippolita as my parents."

"Curse on Hippolita!" cried Manfred. "Forget her from this moment, as I do. In short, Lady, you have missed a husband undeserving of yourcharms: they shall now be better disposed of. Instead of a sicklyboy, you shall have a husband in the prime of his age, who will knowhow to value your beauties, and who may expect a numerous offspring."

"Alas, my Lord!" said Isabella, "my mind is too sadly engrossed by therecent catastrophe in your family to think of another marriage. Ifever my father returns, and it shall be his pleasure, I shall obey, as I did when I consented to give my hand to your son: but until hisreturn, permit me to remain under your hospitable roof, and employ themelancholy hours in assuaging yours, Hippolita's, and the fair Matilda's affliction."

"I desired you once before," said Manfred angrily, "not to name thatwoman: from this hour she must be a stranger to you, as she must beto me. In short, Isabella, since I cannot give you my son, I offer you myself."

"Heavens!" cried Isabella, waking from her delusion, "what do I hear? You! my Lord! You! My father-in-law! the father of Conrad! thehusband of the virtuous and tender Hippolita!"

"I tell you," said Manfred imperiously, "Hippolita is no longer mywife; I divorce her from this hour. Too long has she cursed me by herunfruitfulness. My fate depends on having sons, and this night Itrust will give a new date to my hopes." At those words he seized the cold hand of Isabella, who was half deadwith fright and horror. She shrieked, and started from him, Manfredrose to pursue her, when the moon, which was now up, and gleamed in atthe opposite casement, presented to his sight the plumes of the fatalhelmet, which rose to the height of the windows, waving backwards andforwards in a tempestuous manner, and accompanied with a hollow andrustling sound. Isabella, who gathered courage from her situation,and who dreaded nothing so much as Manfred's pursuit of hisdeclaration, cried -

"Look, my Lord! see, Heaven itself declares against your impiousintentions!"

"Heaven nor Hell shall impede my designs," said Manfred, advancingagain to seize the Princess.

At that instant the portrait of his grandfather, which hung over thebench where they had been sitting, uttered a deep sigh, and heaved its breast.

Isabella, whose back was turned to the picture, saw not the motion,nor knew whence the sound came, but started, and said -

"Hark, my Lord! What sound was that?" and at the same time madetowards the door.

Manfred, distracted between the flight of Isabella, who had nowreached the stairs, and yet unable to keep his eyes from the picture,which began to move, had, however, advanced some steps after her,still looking backwards on the portrait, when he saw it quit itspanel, and descend on the floor with a grave and melancholy air.

"Do I dream?" cried Manfred, returning; "or are the devils themselvesin league against me? Speak, internal spectre! Or, if thou art mygrandsire, why dost thou too conspire against thy wretched descendant,who too dearly pays for - " Ere he could finish the sentence, thevision sighed again, and made a sign to Manfred to follow him.

"Lead on!" cried Manfred; "I will follow thee to the gulf ofperdition."

The spectre marched sedately, but dejected, to the end of the gallery,and turned into a chamber on the right hand. Manfred accompanied himat a little distance, full of anxiety and horror, but resolved. As hewould have entered the chamber, the door was clapped to with violenceby an invisible hand. The Prince, collecting courage from this delay,would have forcibly burst open the door with his foot, but found thatit resisted his utmost efforts.

"Since Hell will not satisfy my curiosity," said Manfred, "I will usethe human means in my power for preserving my race; Isabella shall notescape me."

The lady, whose resolution had given way to terror the moment she hadquitted Manfred, continued her flight to the bottom of the principalstaircase. There she stopped, not knowing whither to direct hersteps, nor how to escape from the impetuosity of the Prince. Thegates of the castle, she knew, were locked, and guards placed in thecourt. Should she, as her heart prompted her, go and prepare Hippolita for the cruel destiny that awaited her, she did not doubtbut Manfred would seek her there, and that his violence would incitehim to double the injury he meditated, without leaving room for themto avoid the impetuosity of his passions. Delay might give him timeto reflect on the horrid measures he had conceived, or produce somecircumstance in her favour, if she could - for that night, at least -avoid his odious purpose. Yet where conceal herself? How avoid thepursuit he would infallibly make throughout the castle?

As these thoughts passed rapidly through her mind, she recollected asubterraneous passage which led from the vaults of the castle to thechurch of St. Nicholas. Could she reach the altar before she wasovertaken, she knew even Manfred's violence would not dare to profanethe sacredness of the place; and she determined, if no other means ofdeliverance offered, to shut herself up for ever among the holyvirgins whose convent was contiguous to the cathedral. In thisresolution, she seized a lamp that burned at the foot of thestaircase, and hurried towards the secret passage.

The lower part of the castle was hollowed into several intricatecloisters; and it was not easy for one under so much anxiety to findthe door that opened into the cavern. An awful silence reignedthroughout those subterraneous regions, except now and then someblasts of wind that shook the doors she had passed, and which, gratingon the rusty hinges, were re-echoed through that long labyrinth ofdarkness. Every murmur struck her with new terror; yet more shedreaded to hear the wrathful voice of Manfred urging his domestics topursue her.

She trod as softly as impatience would give her leave, yet frequentlystopped and listened to hear if she was followed. In one of thosemoments she thought she heard a sigh. She shuddered, and recoiled afew paces. In a moment she thought she heard the step of some person. Her blood curdled; she concluded it was Manfred. Every suggestionthat horror could inspire rushed into her mind. She condemned herrash flight, which had thus exposed her to his rage in a place whereher cries were not likely to draw anybody to her assistance. Yet thesound seemed not to come from behind. If Manfred knew where she was,he must have followed her. She was still in one of the cloisters, andthe steps she had heard were too distinct to proceed from the way shehad come. Cheered with this reflection, and hoping to find a friendin whoever was not the Prince, she was going to advance, when a doorthat stood ajar, at some distance to the left, was opened gently: butere her lamp, which she held up, could discover who opened it, theperson retreated precipitately on seeing the light.

Isabella, whom every incident was sufficient to dismay, hesitatedwhether she should proceed. Her dread of Manfred soon outweighedevery other terror. The very circumstance of the person avoiding hergave her a sort of courage. It could only be, she thought, somedomestic belonging to the castle. Her gentleness had never raised heran enemy, and conscious innocence made her hope that, unless sent bythe Prince's order to seek her, his servants would rather assist thanprevent her flight. Fortifying herself with these reflections, andbelieving by what she could observe that she was near the mouth of thesubterraneous cavern, she approached the door that had been opened;but a sudden gust of wind that met her at the door extinguished herlamp, and left her in total darkness.

Words cannot paint the horror of the Princess's situation. Alone inso dismal a place, her mind imprinted with all the terrible events ofthe day, hopeless of escaping, expecting every moment the arrival of

Manfred, and far from tranquil on knowing she was within reach ofsomebody, she knew not whom, who for some cause seemed concealedthereabouts; all these thoughts crowded on her distracted mind, andshe was ready to sink under her apprehensions. She addressed herselfto every saint in heaven, and inwardly implored their assistance. Fora considerable time she remained in an agony of despair.

At last, as softly as was possible, she felt for the door, and havingfound it, entered trembling into the vault from whence she had heardthe sigh and steps. It gave her a kind of momentary joy to perceivean imperfect ray of clouded moonshine gleam from the roof of thevault, which seemed to be fallen in, and from whence hung a fragmentof earth or building, she could not distinguish which, that appearedto have been crushed inwards. She advanced eagerly towards thischasm, when she discerned a human form standing close against the wall.

She shrieked, believing it the ghost of her betrothed Conrad. Thefigure, advancing, said, in a submissive voice —

"Be not alarmed, Lady; I will not injure you." Isabella, a little encouraged by the words and tone of voice of thestranger, and recollecting that this must be the person who had openedthe door, recovered her spirits enough to reply —

"Sir, whoever you are, take pity on a wretched Princess, standing onthe brink of destruction. Assist me to escape from this fatal castle,or in a few moments I may be made miserable for ever."

"Alas!" said the stranger, "what can I do to assist you? I will diein your defence; but I am unacquainted with the castle, and want—

"Oh!" said Isabella, hastily interrupting him; "help me but to find atrap-door that must be hereabout, and it is the greatest service youcan do me, for I have not a minute to lose."

Saying a these words, she felt about on the pavement, and directed thestranger to search likewise, for a smooth piece of brass enclosed inone of the stones.

"That," said she, "is the lock, which opens with a spring, of which Iknow the secret. If we can find that, I may escape - if not, alas!courteous stranger, I fear I shall have involved you in mymisfortunes: Manfred will suspect you for the accomplice of myflight, and you will fall a victim to his resentment."

"I value not my life," said the stranger, "and it will be some comfortto lose it in trying to deliver you from his tyranny."

"Generous youth," said Isabella, "how shall I ever requite —"

As she uttered those words, a ray of moonshine, streaming through acranny of the ruin above, shone directly on the lock they sought.

"Oh! transport!" said Isabella; "here is the trap-door!" and, takingout the key, she touched the spring, which, starting aside, discoveredan iron ring. "Lift up the door," said the Princess.

The stranger obeyed, and beneath appeared some stone steps descendinginto a vault totally dark.

"We must go down here," said Isabella. "Follow me; dark and dismal asit is, we cannot miss our way; it leads directly to the church of St. Nicholas. But, perhaps," added the Princess modestly, "you have noreason to leave the castle, nor have I farther occasion for yourservice; in a few minutes I shall be safe from Manfred's rage - onlylet me know to whom I am so much obliged."

"I will never quit you," said the stranger eagerly, "until I haveplaced you in safety - nor think me, Princess, more generous than Iam; though you are my principal care - "

The stranger was interrupted by a sudden noise of voices that seemedapproaching, and they soon distinguished these words—

"Talk not to me of necromancers; I tell you she must be in the castle; I will find her in spite of enchantment."

"Oh, heavens!" cried Isabella; "it is the voice of Manfred! Makehaste, or we are ruined! and shut the trap-door after you." Saying this, she descended the steps precipitately; and as thestranger hastened to follow her, he let the door slip out of hishands: it fell, and the spring closed over it. He tried in vain toopen it, not having observed Isabella's method of touching the spring;nor had he many moments to make an essay. The noise of the fallingdoor had been heard by Manfred, who, directed by the sound, hastenedthither, attended by his servants with torches.

"It must be Isabella," cried Manfred, before he entered the vault. "She is escaping by the subterraneous passage, but she cannot have got far.

" What was the astonishment of the Prince when, instead of Isabella, thelight of the torches discovered to him the young peasant whom hethought confined under the fatal helmet!

"Traitor!" said Manfred; "how camest thou here? I thought thee indurance above in the court."

"I am no traitor," replied the young man boldly, "nor am I answerablefor your thoughts."

"Presumptuous villain!" cried Manfred; "dost thou provoke my wrath? Tell me, how hast thou escaped from above? Thou hast corrupted thyguards, and their lives shall answer it."

"My poverty," said the peasant calmly, "will disculpate them: thoughthe ministers of a tyrant's wrath, to thee they are faithful, and buttoo willing to execute the orders which you unjustly imposed upon them."

"Art thou so hardy as to dare my vengeance?" said the Prince; "buttortures shall force the truth from thee. Tell me; I will know thyaccomplices."

"There was my accomplice!" said the youth, smiling, and pointing tothe roof.

Manfred ordered the torches to be held up, and perceived that one ofthe cheeks of the enchanted casque had forced its way through thepavement of the court, as his servants had let it fall over thepeasant, and had broken through into the vault, leaving a gap, throughwhich the peasant had pressed himself some minutes before he was foundby Isabella.

"Was that the way by which thou didst descend?" said Manfred.

"It was," said the youth.

"But what noise was that," said Manfred, "which I heard as I enteredthe cloister?"

"A door clapped," said the peasant; "I heard it as well as you."

"What door?" said Manfred hastily.

"I am not acquainted with your castle," said the peasant; "this is thefirst time I ever entered it, and this vault the only part of itwithin which I ever was."

"But I tell thee," said Manfred (wishing to find out if the youth haddiscovered the trap-door), "it was this way I heard the noise. Myservants heard it too."

"My Lord," interrupted one of them officiously, "to be sure it was thetrap-door, and he was going to make his escape."

"Peace, blockhead!" said the Prince angrily; "if he was going toescape, how should he come on this side? I will know from his ownmouth what noise it was I heard. Tell me truly; thy life depends onthy veracity."

"My veracity is dearer to me than my life," said the peasant; "norwould I purchase the one by forfeiting the other."

"Indeed, young philosopher!" said Manfred contemptuously; "tell me,then, what was the noise I heard?"

"Ask me what I can answer," said he, "and put me to death instantly if I tell you a lie."

Manfred, growing impatient at the steady valour and indifference ofthe youth, cried—

"Well, then, thou man of truth, answer! Was it the fall of the trapdoor that I heard?"

"It was," said the youth.

"It was!" said the Prince; "and how didst thou come to know there wasa trap-door here?"

"I saw the plate of brass by a gleam of moonshine," replied he.

"But what told thee it was a lock?" said Manfred. "How didst thoudiscover the secret of opening it?"

"Providence, that delivered me from the helmet, was able to direct meto the spring of a lock," said he.

"Providence should have gone a little farther, and have placed theeout of the reach of my resentment," said Manfred. "When Providencehad taught thee to open the lock, it abandoned thee for a fool, whodid not know how to make use of its favours. Why didst thou notpursue the path pointed out for thy escape? Why didst thou shut thetrap-door before thou hadst descended the steps?"

"I might ask you, my Lord," said the peasant, "how I, totallyunacquainted with your castle, was to know that those steps led to anyoutlet? but I scorn to evade your questions. Wherever those stepslead to, perhaps I should have explored the way - I could not be in aworse situation than I was. But the truth is, I let the trap-doorfall: your immediate arrival followed. I had given the alarm - whatimported it to me whether I was seized a minute sooner or a minutelater?"

"Thou art a resolute villain for thy years," said Manfred; "yet onreflection I suspect thou dost but trifle with me. Thou hast not yettold me how thou didst open the lock."

"That I will show you, my Lord," said the peasant; and, taking up afragment of stone that had fallen from above, he laid himself on thetrap-door, and began to beat on the piece of brass that covered it,meaning to gain time for the escape of the Princess. This presence ofmind, joined to the frankness of the youth, staggered Manfred. Heeven felt a disposition towards pardoning one who had been guilty ofno crime. Manfred was not one of those savage tyrants who wanton incruelty unprovoked. The circumstances of his fortune had given anasperity to his temper, which was naturally humane; and his virtueswere always ready to operate, when his passions did not obscure his reason.

While the Prince was in this suspense, a confused noise of voicesechoed through the distant vaults. As the sound approached, hedistinguished the clamours of some of his domestics, whom he haddispersed through the castle in search of Isabella, calling out —

"Where is my Lord? where is the Prince?"

"Here I am," said Manfred, as they came nearer; "have you found the Princess?"

The first that arrived, replied, "Oh, my Lord! I am glad we havefound you."

"Found me!" said Manfred; "have you found the Princess?"

"We thought we had, my Lord," said the fellow, looking terrified, "but—

"But, what?" cried the Prince; "has she escaped?"

"Jaquez and I, my Lord - "

"Yes, I and Diego," interrupted the second, who came up in stillgreater consternation.

"Speak one of you at a time," said Manfred; "I ask you, where is the Princess?"

"We do not know," said they both together; "but we are frightened outof our wits."

"So I think, blockheads," said Manfred; "what is it has scared you thus?"

"Oh! my Lord," said Jaquez, "Diego has seen such a sight! your Highness would not believe our eyes."

"What new absurdity is this?" cried Manfred; "give me a direct answer,or, by Heaven — "

"Why, my Lord, if it please your Highness to hear me," said the poorfellow, "Diego and I — "

"Yes, I and Jaquez - " cried his comrade.

"Did not I forbid you to speak both at a time?" said the Prince: "you, Jaquez, answer; for the other fool seems more distracted thanthou art; what is the matter?"

"My gracious Lord," said Jaquez, "if it please your Highness to hearme; Diego and I, according to your Highness's orders, went to searchfor the young Lady; but being comprehensive that we might meet theghost of my young Lord, your Highness's son, God rest his soul, as hehas not received Christian burial - "

"Sot!" cried Manfred in a rage; "is it only a ghost, then, that thou hast seen?"

"Oh! worse! worse! my Lord," cried Diego: "I had rather have seen tenwhole ghosts."

"Grant me patience!" said Manfred; "these blockheads distract me. Outof my sight, Diego! and thou, Jaquez, tell me in one word, art thousober? art thou raving? thou wast wont to have some sense: has theother sot frightened himself and thee too? Speak; what is it hefancies he has seen?"

"Why, my Lord," replied Jaquez, trembling, "I was going to tell your Highness, that since the calamitous misfortune of my young Lord, Godrest his precious soul! not one of us your Highness's faithfulservants - indeed we are, my Lord, though poor men - I say, not one ofus has dared to set a foot about the castle, but two together: so Diego and I, thinking that my young Lady might be in the greatgallery, went up there to look for her, and tell her your Highnesswanted something to impart to her."

"O blundering fools!" cried Manfred; "and in the meantime, she hasmade her escape, because you were afraid of goblins! - Why, thouknave! she left me in the gallery; I came from thence myself."

"For all that, she may be there still for aught I know," said Jaquez; "but the devil shall have me before I seek her there again - poor Diego! I do not believe he will ever recover it."

"Recover what?" said Manfred; "am I never to learn what it is hasterrified these rascals? - but I lose my time; follow me, slave; Iwill see if she is in the gallery."

"For Heaven's sake, my dear, good Lord," cried Jaquez, "do not go tothe gallery. Satan himself I believe is in the chamber next to the gallery."

Manfred, who hitherto had treated the terror of his servants as anidle panic, was struck at this new circumstance. He recollected theapparition of the portrait, and the sudden closing of the door at theend of the gallery. His voice faltered, and he asked with disorder—

"What is in the great chamber?"

"My Lord," said Jaquez, "when Diego and I came into the gallery, hewent first, for he said he had more courage than I. So when we cameinto the gallery we found nobody. We looked under every bench andstool; and still we found nobody."

"Were all the pictures in their places?" said Manfred.

"Yes, my Lord," answered Jaquez; "but we did not think of lookingbehind them."

"Well, well!" said Manfred; "proceed."

"When we came to the door of the great chamber," continued Jaquez, "wefound it shut."

"And could not you open it?" said Manfred.

"Oh! yes, my Lord; would to Heaven we had not!" replied he - "nay, itwas not I neither; it was Diego: he was grown foolhardy, and would goon, though I advised him not - if ever I open a door that is shut again -—"

"Trifle not," said Manfred, shuddering, "but tell me what you saw inthe great chamber on opening the door."

"I! my Lord!" said Jaquez; "I was behind Diego; but I heard the noise."

"Jaquez," said Manfred, in a solemn tone of voice; "tell me, I adjurethee by the souls of my ancestors, what was it thou sawest? what wasit thou heardest?"

"It was Diego saw it, my Lord, it was not I," replied Jaquez; "I onlyheard the noise. Diego had no sooner opened the door, than he criedout, and ran back. I ran back too, and said, 'Is it the ghost?' 'Theghost! no, no,' said Diego, and his hair stood on end - 'it is agiant, I believe; he is all clad in armour, for I saw his foot andpart of his leg, and they are as large as the helmet below in thecourt.' As he said these words, my Lord, we heard a violent motionand the rattling of armour, as if the giant was rising, for Diego hastold me since that he believes the giant was lying down, for the footand leg were stretched at length on the floor. Before we could get tothe end of the gallery, we heard the door of the great chamber clapbehind us, but we did not dare turn back to see if the giant wasfollowing us - yet, now I think on it, we must have heard him if hehad pursued us - but for Heaven's sake, good my Lord, send for thechaplain, and have the castle exorcised, for, for certain, it isenchanted."

"Ay, pray do, my Lord," cried all the servants at once, "or we mustleave your Highness's service."

"Peace, dotards!" said Manfred, "and follow me; I will know what allthis means."

"We! my Lord!" cried they with one voice; "we would not go up to thegallery for your Highness's revenue." The young peasant, who hadstood silent, now spoke.

"Will your Highness," said he, "permit me to try this adventure? Mylife is of consequence to nobody; I fear no bad angel, and haveoffended no good one."

"Your behaviour is above your seeming," said Manfred, viewing him withsurprise and admiration - "hereafter I will reward your bravery - butnow," continued he with a sigh, "I am so circumstanced, that I daretrust no eyes but my own. However, I give you leave to accompany me."

Manfred, when he first followed Isabella from the gallery, had gonedirectly to the apartment of his wife, concluding the Princess hadretired thither. Hippolita, who knew his step, rose with anxiousfondness to meet her Lord, whom she had not seen since the death oftheir son. She would have flown in a transport mixed of joy and griefto his bosom, but he pushed her rudely off, and said—

"Where is Isabella?"

"Isabella! my Lord!" said the astonished Hippolita.

"Yes, Isabella," cried Manfred imperiously; "I want Isabella."

"My Lord," replied Matilda, who perceived how much his behaviour hadshocked her mother, "she has not been with us since your Highnesssummoned her to your apartment."

"Tell me where she is," said the Prince; "I do not want to know whereshe has been."

"My good Lord," says Hippolita, "your daughter tells you the truth: Isabella left us by your command, and has not returned since; - but,my good Lord, compose yourself: retire to your rest: this dismal dayhas disordered you. Isabella shall wait your orders in the morning."

"What, then, you know where she is!" cried Manfred. "Tell medirectly, for I will not lose an instant - and you, woman," speakingto his wife, "order your chaplain to attend me forth with."

"Isabella," said Hippolita calmly, "is retired, I suppose, to herchamber: she is not accustomed to watch at this late hour. Graciousmy Lord," continued she, "let me know what has disturbed you. Has Isabella offended you?"

"Trouble me not with questions," said Manfred, "but tell me where she is."

"Matilda shall call her," said the Princess. "Sit down, my Lord, andresume your wonted fortitude."

"What, art thou jealous of Isabella?" replied he, "that you wish to bepresent at our inter view!"

"Good heavens! my Lord," said Hippolita, "what is it your Highness means?"

"Thou wilt know ere many minutes are passed," said the cruel Prince. "Send your chaplain to me, and wait my pleasure here."

At these words he flung out of the room in search of Isabella, leavingthe amazed ladies thunderstruck with his words and frantic deportment,and lost in vain conjectures on what he was meditating.

Manfred was now returning from the vault, attended by the peasant anda few of his servants whom he had obliged to accompany him. Heascended the staircase without stopping till he arrived at thegallery, at the door of which he met Hippolita and her chaplain. When Diego had been dismissed by Manfred, he had gone directly to the Princess's apartment with the alarm of what he had seen. Thatexcellent Lady, who no more than Manfred doubted of the reality of thevision, yet affected to treat it as a delirium of the servant. Willing, however, to save her Lord from any additional shock, andprepared by a series of griefs not to tremble at any accession to it,she determined to make herself the first sacrifice, if fate had markedthe present hour for their destruction. Dismissing the reluctant Matilda to her rest, who in vain sued for leave to accompany hermother, and attended only by her chaplain, Hippolita had visited thegallery and great chamber; and now with more serenity of soul than shehad felt for many hours, she met her Lord, and assured him that thevision of the gigantic leg and foot was all a fable; and no doubt animpression made by fear, and the dark and dismal hour of the night, onthe minds of his servants. She and the chaplain had examined thechamber, and found everything in the usual order.

Manfred, though persuaded, like his wife, that the vision had been nowork of fancy, recovered a little from the tempest of mind into whichso many strange events had thrown him. Ashamed, too, of his inhumantreatment of a Princess who returned every injury with new marks oftenderness and duty, he felt returning love forcing itself into hiseyes; but not less ashamed of feeling remorse towards one against whomhe was inwardly meditating a yet more bitter outrage, he curbed theyearnings of his heart, and did not dare to lean even towards pity. The next transition of his soul was to exquisite villainy.

Presuming on the unshaken submission of Hippolita, he flatteredhimself that she would not only acquiesce with patience to a divorce,but would obey, if it was his pleasure, in endeavouring to persuade Isabella to give him her hand - but ere he could indulge his horridhope, he reflected that Isabella was not to be found. Coming tohimself, he gave orders that every avenue to the castle should bestrictly guarded, and charged his domestics on pain of their lives tosuffer nobody to pass out. The young peasant, to whom he spokefavourably, he ordered to remain in a small chamber on the stairs, inwhich there was a pallet-bed, and the key of which he took awayhimself, telling the youth he would talk with him in the morning. Then dismissing his attendants, and bestowing a sullen kind of halfnod on Hippolita, he retired to his own chamber.

CHAPTER - II

Matilda, who by Hippolita's order had retired to her apartment, wasill-disposed to take any rest. The shocking fate of her brother haddeeply affected her. She was surprised at not seeing Isabella; butthe strange words which had fallen from her father, and his obscuremenace to the Princess his wife, accompanied by the most furiousbehaviour, had filled her gentle mind with terror and alarm. Shewaited anxiously for the return of Bianca, a young damsel thatattended her, whom she had sent to learn what was become of Isabella. Bianca soon appeared, and informed her mistress of what she hadgathered from the servants, that Isabella was nowhere to be found. She related the adventure of the young peasant who had been discoveredin the vault, though with many simple additions from the incoherentaccounts of the domestics; and she dwelt principally on the giganticleg and foot which had been seen in the gallery-chamber. This lastcircumstance had terrified Bianca so much, that she was rejoiced when Matilda told her that she would not go to rest, but would watch tillthe Princess should rise.

The young Princess wearied herself in conjectures on the flight of Isabella, and on the threats of Manfred to her mother. "But whatbusiness could he have so urgent with the chaplain?"?" said Matilda, "Does he intend to have my brother's body interred privately in the chapel?"

"Oh, Madam!" said Bianca, "now I guess. As you are become hisheiress, he is impatient to have you married: he has always beenraving for more sons; I warrant he is now impatient for grandsons. Assure as I live, Madam, I shall see you a bride at last. - Good madam,you won't cast off your faithful Bianca: you won't put Donna Rosaraover me now you are a great Princess."

"My poor Bianca," said Matilda, "how fast your thoughts amble! I agreat princess! What hast thou seen in Manfred's behaviour since mybrother's death that bespeaks any increase of tenderness to me? No, Bianca; his heart was ever a stranger to me - but he is my father, and I must not complain. Nay, if Heaven shuts my father's heart againstme, it overpays my little merit in the tenderness of my mother - Othat dear mother! yes, Bianca, 'tis there I feel the rugged temper of Manfred. I can support his harshness to me with patience; but itwounds my soul when I am witness to his causeless severity towards her."

"Oh! Madam," said Bianca, "all men use their wives so, when they areweary of them."

"And yet you congratulated me but now," said Matilda, "when youfancied my father intended to dispose of me!"

"I would have you a great Lady," replied Bianca, "come what will. Ido not wish to see you moped in a convent, as you would be if you hadyour will, and if my Lady, your mother, who knows that a bad husbandis better than no husband at all, did not hinder you. - Bless me! whatnoise is that! St. Nicholas forgive me! I was but in jest."

"It is the wind," said Matilda, "whistling through the battlements inthe tower above: you have heard it a thousand times."

"Nay," said Bianca, "there was no harm neither in what I said: it isno sin to talk of matrimony - and so, Madam, as I was saying, if my Lord Manfred should offer you a handsome young Prince for abridegroom, you would drop him a curtsey, and tell him you wouldrather take the veil?"

"Thank Heaven! I am in no such danger," said Matilda: "you know howmany proposals for me he has rejected— "

"And you thank him, like a dutiful daughter, do you, Madam? But come, Madam; suppose, to-morrow morning, he was to send for you to the greatcouncil chamber, and there you should find at his elbow a lovely youngb Prince, with large black eyes, a smooth white forehead, and manlycurling locks like jet; in short, Madam, a young hero resembling thepicture of the good Alfonso in the gallery, which you sit and gaze atfor hours together — "

"Do not speak lightly of that picture," interrupted Matilda sighing; "I know the adoration with which I look at that picture is uncommon -

but I am not in love with a coloured panel. The character of thatvirtuous Prince, the veneration with which my mother has inspired mefor his memory, the orisons which, I know not why, she has enjoined meto pour forth at his tomb, all have concurred to persuade me thatsomehow or other my destiny is linked with something relating to him."

"Lord, Madam! how should that be?" said Bianca; "I have always heardthat your family was in no way related to his: and I am sure I cannotconceive why my Lady, the Princess, sends you in a cold morning or adamp evening to pray at his tomb: he is no saint by the almanack. Ifyou must pray, why does she not bid you address yourself to our great St. Nicholas? I am sure he is the saint I pray to for a husband."

"Perhaps my mind would be less affected," said Matilda, "if my motherwould explain her reasons to me: but it is the mystery she observes,that inspires me with this - I know not what to call it. As she neveracts from caprice, I am sure there is some fatal secret at bottom - nay, I know there is: in her agony of grief for my brother's deathshe dropped some words that intimated as much."

"Oh! dear Madam," cried Bianca, "what were they?"

"No," said Matilda, "if a parent lets fall a word, and wishes itrecalled, it is not for a child to utter it."

"What! was she sorry for what she had said?" asked Bianca; "I am sure, Madam, you may trust me—"

"With my own little secrets when I have any, I may," said Matilda; "but never with my mother's: a child ought to have no ears or eyesbut as a parent directs."

"Well! to be sure, Madam, you were born to be a saint," said Bianca, "and there is no resisting one's vocation: you will end in a conventat last. But there is my Lady Isabella would not be so reserved tome: she will let me talk to her of young men: and when a handsomecavalier has come to the castle, she has owned to me that she wishedyour brother Conrad resembled him."

"Bianca," said the Princess, "I do not allow you to mention my frienddisrespectfully. Isabella is of a cheerful disposition, but her soulis pure as virtue itself. She knows your idle babbling humour, andperhaps has now and then encouraged it, to divert melancholy, andenliven the solitude in which my father keeps us — "

"Blessed Mary!" said Bianca, starting, "there it is again! Dear Madam, do you hear nothing? this castle is certainly haunted!"

"Peace!" said Matilda, "and listen! I did think I heard a voice - butit must be fancy: your terrors, I suppose, have infected me."

"Indeed! indeed! Madam," said Bianca, half-weeping with agony, "I amsure I heard a voice."

"Does anybody lie in the chamber beneath?" said the Princess.

"Nobody has dared to lie there," answered Bianca, "since the greatastrologer, that was your brother's tutor, drowned himself. Forcertain, Madam, his ghost and the young Prince's are now met in thechamber below - for Heaven's sake let us fly to your mother's apartment!"

"I charge you not to stir," said Matilda. "If they are spirits inpain, we may ease their sufferings by questioning them. They can meanno hurt to us, for we have not injured them - and if they should,shall we be more safe in one chamber than in another? Reach me mybeads; we will say a prayer, and then speak to them."

"Oh! dear Lady, I would not speak to a ghost for the world!" cried Bianca. As she said those words they heard the casement of the littlechamber below Matilda's open. They listened attentively, and in a fewminutes thought they heard a person sing, but could not distinguishthe words.

"This can be no evil spirit," said the Princess, in a low voice; "itis undoubtedly one of the family - open the window, and we shall know the voice."

"I dare not, indeed, Madam," said Bianca.

"Thou art a very fool," said Matilda, opening the window gentlyherself. The noise the Princess made was, however, heard by theperson beneath, who stopped; and they concluded had heard the casement open.

“Is anybody below?” said the Princess; “if there is, speak.”

“Yes,” said an unknown voice.

“Who is it?” said Matilda.

“A stranger,” replied the voice.

“What stranger?” said she; “and how didst thou come there at thisunusual hour, when all the gates of the castle are locked?”

“I am not here willingly,” answered the voice. “But pardon me, Lady,if I have disturbed your rest; I knew not that I was overheard. Sleephad forsaken me; I left a restless couch, and came to waste theirksome hours with gazing on the fair approach of morning, impatientto be dismissed from this castle.”

“Thy words and accents,” said Matilda, “are of melancholy cast; ifthou art unhappy, I pity thee. If poverty afflicts thee, let me knowit; I will mention thee to the Princess, whose beneficent soul evermelts for the distressed, and she will relieve thee.”

“I am indeed unhappy,” said the stranger; “and I know not what wealthis. But I do not complain of the lot which Heaven has cast for me; Iam young and healthy, and am not ashamed of owing my support to myself"

- yet think me not proud, or that I disdain your generous offers. Iwill remember you in my orisons, and will pray for blessings on yourgracious self and your noble mistress - if I sigh, Lady, it is forothers, not for myself.”

“Now I have it, Madam,” said Bianca, whispering the Princess; “this iscertainly the young peasant; and, by my conscience, he is in love -Well! this is a charming adventure! - do, Madam, let us sift him. Hedoes not know you, but takes you for one of my Lady Hippolita’s women.”

“Art thou not ashamed, Bianca!” said the Princess. “What right havewe to pry into the secrets of this young man’s heart? He seemsvirtuous and frank, and tells us he is unhappy. Are thosecircumstances that authorise us to make a property of him? How are weentitled to his confidence?”

"Lord, Madam! how little you know of love!" replied Bianca; "why,lovers have no pleasure equal to talking of their mistress."

"And would you have ME become a peasant's confidante?" said the Princess.

"Well, then, let me talk to him," said Bianca; "though I have thehonour of being your Highness's maid of honour, I was not always sogreat. Besides, if love levels ranks, it raises them too; I have arespect for any young man in love."

"Peace, simpleton!" said the Princess. "Though he said he wasunhappy, it does not follow that he must be in love. Think of allthat has happened to-day, and tell me if there are no misfortunes butwhat love causes. - Stranger," resumed the Princess, "if thymisfortunes have not been occasioned by thy own fault, and are withinthe compass of the Princess Hippolita's power to redress, I will takeupon me to answer that she will be thy protectress. When thou artdismissed from this castle, repair to holy father Jerome, at theconvent adjoining to the church of St. Nicholas, and make thy storyknown to him, as far as thou thinkest meet. He will not fail toinform the Princess, who is the mother of all that want herassistance. Farewell; it is not seemly for me to hold fartherconverse with a man at this unwonted hour."

"May the saints guard thee, gracious Lady!" replied the peasant; "butoh! if a poor and worthless stranger might presume to beg a minute'saudience farther; am I so happy? the casement is not shut; might Iventure to ask—"

"Speak quickly," said Matilda; "the morning dawns apace: should thelabourers come into the fields and perceive us - What wouldst thou ask?"

"I know not how, I know not if I dare," said the Young stranger,faltering; "yet the humanity with which you have spoken to meemboldens - Lady! dare I trust you?"

"Heavens!" said Matilda, "what dost thou mean? With what wouldst thoutrust me? Speak boldly, if thy secret is fit to be entrusted to a virtuous breast."

"I would ask," said the peasant, recollecting himself, "whether what Ihave heard from the domestics is true, that the Princess is missingfrom the castle?"

"What imports it to thee to know?" replied Matilda."Thy first words bespoke a prudent and becoming gravity. Dost thou come hither to pryinto the secrets of Manfred? Adieu. I have been mistaken in thee." Saying these words she shut the casement hastily, without giving theyoung man time to reply.

"I had acted more wisely," said the Princess to Bianca, with somesharpness, "if I had let thee converse with this peasant; hisinquisitiveness seems of a piece with thy own."

"It is not fit for me to argue with your Highness," replied Bianca; "but perhaps the questions I should have put to him would have beenmore to the purpose than those you have been pleased to ask him."

"Oh! no doubt," said Matilda; "you are a very discreet personage! May I know what YOU would have asked him?"

"A bystander often sees more of the game than those that play,"answered Bianca. "Does your Highness think, Madam, that this questionabout my Lady Isabella was the result of mere curiosity? No, no, Madam, there is more in it than you great folks are aware of. Lopeztold me that all the servants believe this young fellow contrived my Lady Isabella's escape; now, pray, Madam, observe you and I both knowthat my Lady Isabella never much fancied the Prince your brother. Well! he is killed just in a critical minute - I accuse nobody. Ahelmet falls from the moon - so, my Lord, your father says; but Lopezand all the servants say that this young spark is a magician, andstole it from Alfonso's tomb—"

"Have done with this rhapsody of impertinence," said Matilda.

"Nay, Madam, as you please," cried Bianca; "yet it is very particularthough, that my Lady Isabella should be missing the very same day, andthat this young sorcerer should be found at the mouth of the trapdoor. I accuse nobody; but if my young Lord came honestly by hisdeath—"

"Dare not on thy duty," said Matilda, "to breathe a suspicion on thepurity of my dear Isabella's fame."

"Purity, or not purity," said Bianca, "gone she is - a stranger isfound that nobody knows; you question him yourself; he tells you he isin love, or unhappy, it is the same thing - nay, he owned he wasunhappy about others; and is anybody unhappy about another, unlessthey are in love with them? and at the very next word, he asksinnocently, pour soul! if my Lady Isabella is missing."

"To be sure," said Matilda, "thy observations are not totally withoutfoundation - Isabella's flight amazes me. The curiosity of thestranger is very particular; yet Isabella never concealed a thoughtfrom me."

"So she told you," said Bianca, "to fish out your secrets; but whoknows, Madam, but this stranger may be some Prince in disguise? Do, Madam, let me open the window, and ask him a few questions."

"No," replied Matilda, "I will ask him myself, if he knows aught of Isabella; he is not worthy I should converse farther with him." Shewas going to open the casement, when they heard the bell ring at thepostern-gate of the castle, which is on the right hand of the tower,where Matilda lay. This prevented the Princess from renewing theconversation with the stranger.

After continuing silent for some time, "I am persuaded," said she to Bianca, "that whatever be the cause of Isabella's flight it had nounworthy motive. If this stranger was accessory to it, she must besatisfied with his fidelity and worth. I observed, did not you, Bianca? that his words were tinctured with an uncommon infusion ofpiety. It was no ruffian's speech; his phrases were becoming a man of gentle birth."

"I told you, Madam," said Bianca, "that I was sure he was some Princein disguise."

"Yet," said Matilda, "if he was privy to her escape, how will youaccount for his not accompanying her in her flight? why expose himselfunnecessarily and rashly to my father's resentment?"

"As for that, Madam," replied she, "if he could get from under thehelmet, he will find ways of eluding your father's anger. I do notdoubt but he has some talisman or other about him."

"You resolve everything into magic," said Matilda; "but a man who hasany intercourse with infernal spirits, does not dare to make use ofthose tremendous and holy words which he uttered. Didst thou notobserve with what fervour he vowed to remember ME to heaven in hisprayers? Yes; Isabella was undoubtedly convinced of his piety."

"Commend me to the piety of a young fellow and a damsel that consultto elope!" said Bianca. "No, no, Madam, my Lady Isabella is ofanother guess mould than you take her for. She used indeed to sighand lift up her eyes in your company, because she knows you are asaint; but when your back was turned — "

"You wrong her," said Matilda; "Isabella is no hypocrite; she has adue sense of devotion, but never affected a call she has not. On thecontrary, she always combated my inclination for the cloister; andthough I own the mystery she has made to me of her flight confoundsme; though it seems inconsistent with the friendship between us; Icannot forget the disinterested warmth with which she always opposedmy taking the veil. She wished to see me married, though my dowerwould have been a loss to her and my brother's children. For her sake I will believe well of this young peasant."

"Then you do think there is some liking between them," said Bianca. While she was speaking, a servant came hastily into the chamber andtold the Princess that the Lady Isabella was found.

"Where?" said Matilda.

"She has taken sanctuary in St. Nicholas's church," replied theservant; "Father Jerome has brought the news himself; he is below withhis Highness."

"Where is my mother?" said Matilda.

"She is in her own chamber, Madam, and has asked for you."

Manfred had risen at the first dawn of light, and gone to Hippolita'sapartment, to inquire if she knew aught of Isabella. While he wasquestioning her, word was brought that Jerome demanded to speak withhim. Manfred, little suspecting the cause of the Friar's arrival, andknowing he was employed by Hippolita in her charities, ordered him tobe admitted, intending to leave them together, while he pursued hissearch after Isabella.

"Is your business with me or the Princess?" said Manfred.

"With both," replied the holy man. "The Lady Isabella - "

"What of her?" interrupted Manfred, eagerly.

"Is at St. Nicholas's altar," replied Jerome.

"That is no business of Hippolita," said Manfred with confusion; "letus retire to my chamber, Father, and inform me how she came thither."

"No, my Lord," replied the good man, with an air of firmness andauthority, that daunted even the resolute Manfred, who could not helprevering the saint-like virtues of Jerome; "my commission is to both,and with your Highness's good-liking, in the presence of both I shalldeliver it; but first, my Lord, I must interrogate the Princess,whether she is acquainted with the cause of the Lady Isabella'sretirement from your castle."

"No, on my soul," said Hippolita; "does Isabella charge me with beingprivy to it?"

"Father," interrupted Manfred, "I pay due reverence to your holyprofession; but I am sovereign here, and will allow no meddling priestto interfere in the affairs of my domestic. If you have aught to sayattend me to my chamber; I do not use to let my wife be acquaintedwith the secret affairs of my state; they are not within a woman's province."

"My Lord," said the holy man, "I am no intruder into the secrets offamilies. My office is to promote peace, to heal divisions, to preachrepentance, and teach mankind to curb their headstrong passions. Iforgive your Highness's uncharitable apostrophe; I know my duty, andam the minister of a mightier prince than Manfred. Hearken to him whospeaks through my organs."

Manfred trembled with rage and shame. Hippolita's countenancedeclared her astonishment and impatience to know where this would end. Her silence more strongly spoke her observance of Manfred.

"The Lady Isabella," resumed Jerome, "commends herself to both your Highnesses; she thanks both for the kindness with which she has beentreated in your castle: she deplores the loss of your son, and herown misfortune in not becoming the daughter of such wise and noble Princes, whom she shall always respect as Parents; she prays foruninterrupted union and felicity between you" [Manfred's colourchanged]: "but as it is no longer possible for her to be allied toyou, she entreats your consent to remain in sanctuary, till she canlearn news of her father, or, by the certainty of his death, be atliberty, with the approbation of her guardians, to dispose of herselfin suitable marriage."

"I shall give no such consent," said the Prince, "but insist on herreturn to the castle without delay: I am answerable for her person toher guardians, and will not brook her being in any hands but my own."

"Your Highness will recollect whether that can any longer be proper,"replied the Friar.

"I want no monitor," said Manfred, colouring; "Isabella's conductleaves room for strange suspicions - and that young villain, who wasat least the accomplice of her flight, if not the cause of it— "

"The cause!" interrupted Jerome; "was a *Young* man the cause?"

"This is not to be borne!" cried Manfred. "Am I to be bearded in myown palace by an insolent Monk? Thou art privy, I guess, to their amours."

"I would pray to heaven to clear up your uncharitable surmises," said Jerome, "if your Highness were not satisfied in your conscience howunjustly you accuse me. I do pray to heaven to pardon thatuncharitableness: and I implore your Highness to leave the Princessat peace in that holy place, where she is not liable to be disturbedby such vain and worldly fantasies as discourses of love from any man."

"Cant not to me," said Manfred, "but return and bring the Princess toher duty."

"It is my duty to prevent her return hither," said Jerome. "She iswhere orphans and virgins are safest from the snares and wiles of thisworld; and nothing but a parent's authority shall take her thence."

"I am her parent," cried Manfred, "and demand her."

"She wished to have you for her parent," said the Friar; "but Heaventhat forbad that connection has for ever dissolved all ties betwixtyou: and I announce to your Highness—"

"Stop! audacious man," said Manfred, "and dread my displeasure."

"Holy farther," said Hippolita, "it is your office to be no respecterof persons: you must speak as your duty prescribes: but it is myduty to hear nothing that it pleases not my Lord I should hear. Attend the Prince to his chamber. I will retire to my oratory, andpray to the blessed Virgin to inspire you with her holy counsels, andto restore the heart of my gracious Lord to its wonted peace and gentleness."

"Excellent woman!" said the Friar."My Lord, I attend your pleasure."

Manfred, accompanied by the Friar, passed to his own apartment, whereshutting the door, "I perceive, Father," said he, "that Isabella hasacquainted you with my purpose. Now hear my resolve, and obey. Reasons of state, most urgent reasons, my own and the safety of mypeople, demand that I should have a son. It is in vain to expect anheir from Hippolita. I have made choice of Isabella. You must bringher back; and you must do more. I know the influence you have with Hippolita: her conscience is in your hands. She is, I allow, afaultless woman: her soul is set on heaven, and scorns the littlegrandeur of this world: you can withdraw her from it entirely.

Persuade her to consent to the dissolution of our marriage, and toretire into a monastery - she shall endow one if she will; and sheshall have the means of being as liberal to your order as she or youcan wish. Thus you will divert the calamities that are hanging overour heads, and have the merit of saying the principality of Otrantofrom destruction. You are a prudent man, and though the warmth of mytemper betrayed me into some unbecoming expressions, I honour yourvirtue, and wish to be indebted to you for the repose of my life andthe preservation of my family."

"The will of heaven be done!" said the Friar. "I am but its worthlessinstrument. It makes use of my tongue to tell thee, Prince, of thyunwarrantable designs. The injuries of the virtuous Hippolita havemounted to the throne of pity. By me thou art reprimanded for thyadulterous intention of repudiating her: by me thou art warned not topursue the incestuous design on thy contracted daughter. Heaven thatdelivered her from thy fury, when the judgments so recently fallen onthy house ought to have inspired thee with other thoughts, willcontinue to watch over her. Even I, a poor and despised Friar, amable to protect her from thy violence - I, sinner as I am, anduncharitably reviled by your Highness as an accomplice of I know notwhat amours, scorn the allurements with which it has pleased thee totempt mine honesty. I love my order; I honour devout souls; I respectthe piety of thy Princess - but I will not betray the confidence shereposes in me, nor serve even the cause of religion by foul and sinfulcompliances - but forsooth! the welfare of the state depends on your Highness having a son! Heaven mocks the short-sighted views of man. But yester-morn, whose house was so great, so flourishing as Manfred's? - where is young Conrad now? - My Lord, I respect yourtears - but I mean not to check them - let them flow, Prince! Theywill weigh more with heaven toward the welfare of thy subjects, than amarriage, which, founded on lust or policy, could never prosper. Thesceptre, which passed from the race of Alfonso to thine, cannot bepreserved by a match which the church will never allow. If it is thewill of the Most High that Manfred's name must perish, resignyourself, my Lord, to its decrees; and thus deserve a crown that cannever pass away. Come, my Lord; I like this sorrow - let us return tothe Princess: she is not apprised of your cruel intentions; nor did Imean more than to alarm you. You saw with what gentle patience, withwhat efforts of love, she heard, she rejected hearing, the extent ofyour guilt. I know she longs to fold you in her arms, and assure youof her unalterable affection."

"Father," said the Prince, "you mistake my compunction: true, Ihonour Hippolita's virtues; I think her a Saint; and wish it were formy soul's health to tie faster the knot that has united us - but alas! Father, you know not the bitterest of my pangs! it is some time that Ihave had scruples on the legality of our union: Hippolita is relatedto me in the fourth degree - it is true, we had a dispensation: but Ihave been informed that she had also been contracted to another. Thisit is that sits heavy at my heart: to this state of unlawful wedlock I impute the visitation that has fallen on me in the death of Conrad !—ease my conscience of this burden: dissolve our marriage, andaccomplish the work of godliness - which your divine exhortations havecommenced in my soul."

How cutting was the anguish which the good man felt, when he perceivedthis turn in the wily Prince! He trembled for Hippolita, whose ruinhe saw was determined; and he feared if Manfred had no hope ofrecovering Isabella, that his impatience for a son would direct him tosome other object, who might not be equally proof against thetemptation of Manfred's rank. For some time the holy man remainedabsorbed in thought. At length, conceiving some hopes from delay, hethought the wisest conduct would be to prevent the Prince fromdespairing of recovering Isabella. Her the Friar knew he coulddispose, from her affection to Hippolita, and from the aversion shehad expressed to him for Manfred's addresses, to second his views,till the censures of the church could be fulminated against a divorce. With this intention, as if struck with the Prince's scruples, he atlength said:

"My Lord, I have been pondering on what your Highness has said; and ifin truth it is delicacy of conscience that is the real motive of yourrepugnance to your virtuous Lady, far be it from me to endeavour toharden your heart. The church is an indulgent mother: unfold yourgriefs to her: she alone can administer comfort to your soul, eitherby satisfying your conscience, or upon examination of your scruples,by setting you at liberty, and indulging you in the lawful means ofcontinuing your lineage. In the latter case, if the Lady Isabella canbe brought to consent— "

Manfred, who concluded that he had either over-reached the good man,or that his first warmth had been but a tribute paid to appearance,was overjoyed at this sudden turn, and repeated the most magnificentpromises, if he should succeed by the Friar's mediation. The wellmeaning priest suffered him to deceive himself, fully determined totraverse his views, instead of seconding them.

"Since we now understand one another," resumed the Prince, "I expect, Father, that you satisfy me in one point. Who is the youth that

Ifound in the vault? He must have been privy to Isabella's flight:tell me truly, is he her lover? or is he an agent for another'spassion? I have often suspected Isabella's indifference to my son: athousand circumstances crowd on my mind that confirm that suspicion. She herself was so conscious of it, that while I discoursed her in thegallery, she outran my suspicious, and endeavoured to justify herselffrom coolness to Conrad."

The Friar, who knew nothing of the youth, but what he had learntoccasionally from the Princess, ignorant what was become of him, andnot sufficiently reflecting on the impetuosity of Manfred's temper,conceived that it might not be amiss to sow the seeds of jealousy inhis mind: they might be turned to some use hereafter, either byprejudicing the Prince against Isabella, if he persisted in that unionor by diverting his attention to a wrong scent, and employing histhoughts on a visionary intrigue, prevent his engaging in any newpursuit. With this unhappy policy, he answered in a manner to confirm Manfred in the belief of some connection between Isabella and theyouth. The Prince, whose passions wanted little fuel to throw theminto a blaze, fell into a rage at the idea of what the Friar suggested.

"I will fathom to the bottom of this intrigue," cried he; andquitting Jerome abruptly, with a command to remain there till hisreturn, he hastened to the great hall of the castle, and ordered thepeasant to be brought before him.

"Thou hardened young impostor!" said the Prince, as soon as he saw theyouth; "what becomes of thy boasted veracity now? it was Providence,was it, and the light of the moon, that discovered the lock of thetrap-door to thee? Tell me, audacious boy, who thou art, and how longthou hast been acquainted with the Princess - and take care to answerwith less equivocation than thou didst last night, or tortures shallwring the truth from thee."

The young man, perceiving that his share in the flight of the Princesswas discovered, and concluding that anything he should say could nolonger be of any service or detriment to her, replied—

"I am no impostor, my Lord, nor have I deserved opprobrious language. I answered to every question your Highness put to me last night withthe same veracity that I shall speak now: and that will not be fromfear of your tortures, but because my soul abhors a falsehood. Pleaseto repeat your questions, my Lord; I am ready to give you all thesatisfaction in my power."

"You know my questions," replied the Prince, "and only want time toprepare an evasion. Speak directly; who art thou? and how long hastthou been known to the Princess?"

"I am a labourer at the next village," said the peasant; "my name is

Theodore. The Princess found me in the vault last night: before thathour I never was in her presence."

"I may believe as much or as little as I please of this," said Manfred; "but I will hear thy own story before I examine into thetruth of it. Tell me, what reason did the Princess give thee formaking her escape? thy life depends on thy answer."

"She told me," replied Theodore, "that she was on the brink ofdestruction, and that if she could not escape from the castle, she wasin danger in a few moments of being made miserable for ever."

"And on this slight foundation, on a silly girl's report," said Manfred, "thou didst hazard my displeasure?"

"I fear no man's displeasure," said Theodore, "when a woman indistress puts herself under my protection."

During this examination, Matilda was going to the apartment of Hippolita. At the upper end of the hall, where Manfred sat, was aboarded gallery with latticed windows, through which Matilda and Bianca were to pass. Hearing her father's voice, and seeing theservants assembled round him, she stopped to learn the occasion. Theprisoner soon drew her attention: the steady and composed manner inwhich he answered, and the gallantry of his last reply, which were thefirst words she heard distinctly, interested her in his flavour. Hisperson was noble, handsome, and commanding, even in that situation:but his countenance soon engrossed her whole care.

"Heavens! Bianca," said the Princess softly, "do I dream? or is notthat youth the exact resemblance of Alfonso's picture in the gallery?"

She could say no more, for her father's voice grew louder at every word.

"This bravado,"said he, "surpasses all thy former insolence. Thoushalt experience the wrath with which thou darest to trifle. Seizehim," continued Manfred, "and 'bind him - the first news the Princesshears of her champion shall be, that he has lost his head for hersake."

"The injustice of which thou art guilty towards me," said Theodore, "convinces me that I have done a good deed in delivering the Princessfrom thy tyranny. May she be happy, whatever becomes of me!"

"This is a lover!" cried Manfred in a rage: "a peasant within sightof death is not animated by such sentiments. Tell me, tell me, rashboy, who thou art, or the rack shall force thy secret from thee."

"Thou hast threatened me with death already," said the youth, "for thetruth I have told thee: if that is all the encouragement I am toexpect for sincerity, I am not tempted to indulge thy vain curiosity farther."

"Then thou wilt not speak?" said Manfred.

"I will not," replied he.

"Bear him away into the courtyard," said Manfred; "I will see his headthis instant severed from his body."

Matilda fainted at hearing those words. Bianca shrieked, and cried

"Help! help! the Princess is dead!" Manfred started at thisejaculation, and demanded what was the matter! The young peasant, whoheard it too, was struck with horror, and asked eagerly the samequestion; but Manfred ordered him to be hurried into the court, andkept there for execution, till he had informed himself of the cause of Bianca's shrieks. When he learned the meaning, he treated it as awomanish panic, and ordering Matilda to be carried to her apartment,he rushed into the court, and calling for one of his guards, bade Theodore kneel down, and prepare to receive the fatal blow.

The undaunted youth received the bitter sentence with a resignationthat touched every heart but Manfred's. He wished earnestly to knowthe meaning of the words he had heard relating to the Princess;

butfearing to exasperate the tyrant more against her, he desisted. Theonly boon he deigned to ask was, that he might be permitted to have aconfessor, and make his peace with heaven. Manfred, who hoped by theconfessor's means to come at the youth's history, readily granted hisrequest; and being convinced that Father Jerome was now in hisinterest, he ordered him to be called and shrive the prisoner. Theholy man, who had little foreseen the catastrophe that his imprudenceoccasioned, fell on his knees to the Prince, and adjured him in themost solemn manner not to shed innocent blood. He accused himself inthe bitterest terms for his indiscretion, endeavoured to disculpatethe youth, and left no method untried to soften the tyrant's rage. Manfred, more incensed than appeased by Jerome's intercession, whoseretraction now made him suspect he had been imposed upon by both,commanded the Friar to do his duty, telling him he would not allow theprisoner many minutes for confession.

"Nor do I ask many, my Lord," said the unhappy young man. "My sins,thank heaven, have not been numerous; nor exceed what might beexpected at my years. Dry your tears, good Father, and let usdespatch. This is a bad world; nor have I had cause to leave it with regret."

"Oh wretched youth!" said Jerome; "how canst thou bear the sight of mewith patience? I am thy murderer! it is I have brought this dismalhour upon thee!"

"I forgive thee from my soul," said the youth, "as I hope heaven willpardon me. Hear my confession, Father; and give me thy blessing."

"How can I prepare thee for thy passage as I ought?" said Jerome. "Thou canst not be saved without pardoning thy foes - and canst thouforgive that impious man there?"

"I can," said Theodore; "I do."

"And does not this touch thee, cruel Prince?" said the Friar.

"I sent for thee to confess him," said Manfred, sternly; "not to pleadfor him. Thou didst first incense me against him - his blood be uponthy head!"

"It will! it will!" said the good main, in an agony of sorrow. "Thouand I must never hope to go where this blessed youth is going!"

"Despatch!" said Manfred; "I am no more to be moved by the whining ofpriests than by the shrieks of women."

"What!" said the youth; "is it possible that my fate could haveoccasioned what I heard! Is the Princess then again in thy power?"

"Thou dost but remember me of my wrath," said Manfred. "Prepare thee,for this moment is thy last."

The youth, who felt his indignation rise, and who was touched with thesorrow which he saw he had infused into all the spectators, as well asinto the Friar, suppressed his emotions, and putting off his doublet,and unbuttoning, his collar, knelt down to his prayers. As hestooped, his shirt slipped down below his shoulder, and discovered themark of a bloody arrow.

"Gracious heaven!" cried the holy man, starting; "what do I see? Itis my child! my Theodore!"

The passions that ensued must be conceived; they cannot be painted. The tears of the assistants were suspended by wonder, rather thanstopped by joy. They seemed to inquire in the eyes of their Lord whatthey ought to feel. Surprise, doubt, tenderness, respect, succeededeach other in the countenance of the youth. He received with modestsubmission the effusion of the old man's tears and embraces. Yetafraid of giving a loose to hope, and suspecting from what had passedthe inflexibility of Manfred's temper, he cast a glance towards the Prince, as if to say, canst thou be unmoved at such a scene as this?

Manfred's heart was capable of being touched. He forgot his anger inhis astonishment; yet his pride forbad his owning himself affected. He even doubted whether this discovery was not a contrivance of the Friar to save the youth.

"What may this mean?" said he. "How can he be thy son? Is itconsistent with thy profession or reputed sanctity to avow a peasant'soffspring for the fruit of thy irregular amours!"

"Oh, God!" said the holy man, "dost thou question his being mine? Could I feel the anguish I do if I were not his father? Spare him!good Prince! spare him! and revile me as thou pleasest."

"Spare him! spare him!" cried the attendants; "for this good man'ssake!"

"Peace!" said Manfred, sternly. "I must know more ere I am disposedto pardon. A Saint's bastard may be no saint himself."

"Injurious Lord!" said Theodore, "add not insult to cruelty. If I amthis venerable man's son, though no Prince, as thou art, know theblood that flows in my veins—"

"Yes," said the Friar, interrupting him, "his blood is noble; nor ishe that abject thing, my Lord, you speak him. He is my lawful son,and Sicily can boast of few houses more ancient than that of Falconara. But alas! my Lord, what is blood! what is nobility! Weare all reptiles, miserable, sinful creatures. It is piety alone thatcan distinguish us from the dust whence we sprung, and whither we must return."

"Truce to your sermon," said Manfred; "you forget you are no longer Friar Jerome, but the Count of Falconara. Let me know your history;you will have time to moralise hereafter, if you should not happen toobtain the grace of that sturdy criminal there."

"Mother of God!" said the Friar, "is it possible my Lord can refuse afather the life of his only, his long-lost, child! Trample me, my Lord, scorn, afflict me, accept my life for his, but spare my son!"

"Thou canst feel, then," said Manfred, "what it is to lose an onlyson! A little hour ago thou didst preach up resignation to me: MYhouse, if fate so pleased, must perish - but the Count of Falconara—"

"Alas! my Lord," said Jerome, "I confess I have offended; butaggravate not an old man's sufferings! I boast not of my family, northink of such vanities - it is nature, that pleads for this boy; it is the memory of the dear woman that bore him. Is she, Theodore, is she dead?"

"Her soul has long been with the blessed," said Theodore.

"Oh! how?" cried Jerome, "tell me - no - she is happy! Thou art allmy care now! - Most dread Lord! will you - will you grant me my poorboy's life?"

"Return to thy convent," answered Manfred; "conduct the Princesshither; obey me in what else thou knowest; and I promise thee the lifeof thy son."

"Oh! my Lord," said Jerome, "is my honesty the price I must pay forthis dear youth's safety?"

"For me!" cried Theodore. "Let me die a thousand deaths, rather thanstain thy conscience. What is it the tyrant would exact of thee? Isthe Princess still safe from his power? Protect her, thou venerableold man; and let all the weight of his wrath fall on me."

Jerome endeavoured to check the impetuosity of the youth; and ere Manfred could reply, the trampling of horses was heard, and a brazentrumpet, which hung without the gate of the castle, was suddenlysounded. At the same instant the sable plumes on the enchantedhelmet, which still remained at the other end of the court, weretempestuously agitated, and nodded thrice, as if bowed by someinvisible wearer.

CHAPTER - III

Manfred's heart misgave him when he beheld the plumage on themiraculous casque shaken in concert with the sounding of the brazen trumpet.

"Father!" said he to Jerome, whom he now ceased to treat as Count of

Falconara, "what mean these portents? If I have offended—" the plumes were shaken with greater violence than before.

"Unhappy Prince that I am," cried Manfred. "Holy Father! will you notassist me with your prayers?"

"My Lord," replied Jerome, "heaven is no doubt displeased with yourmockery of its servants. Submit yourself to the church; and cease topersecute her ministers. Dismiss this innocent youth; and learn torespect the holy character I wear. Heaven will not be trifled with:you see - " the trumpet sounded again.

"I acknowledge I have been too hasty," said Manfred. "Father, do yougo to the wicket, and demand who is at the gate."

"Do you grant me the life of Theodore?" replied the Friar.

"I do," said Manfred; "but inquire who is without!"

Jerome, falling on the neck of his son, discharged a flood of tears,that spoke the fulness of his soul.

"You promised to go to the gate," said Manfred.

"I thought," replied the Friar, "your Highness would excuse mythanking you first in this tribute of my heart."

"Go, dearest Sir," said Theodore; "obey the Prince. I do not deservethat you should delay his satisfaction for me."

Jerome, inquiring who was without, was answered, "A Herald."

"From whom?" said he.

"From the Knight of the Gigantic Sabre," said the Herald; "and I mustspeak with the usurper of Otranto."

Jerome returned to the Prince, and did not fail to repeat the messagein the very words it had been uttered. The first sounds struck

Manfred with terror; but when he heard himself styled usurper, hisrage rekindled, and all his courage revived.

"Usurper! - insolent villain!" cried he; "who dares to question mytitle? Retire, Father; this is no business for Monks: I will meetthis presumptuous man myself. Go to your convent and prepare the Princess's return. Your son shall be a hostage for your fidelity:his life depends on your obedience."

"Good heaven! my Lord," cried Jerome, "your Highness did but thisinstant freely pardon my child - have you so soon forgot theinterposition of heaven?"

"Heaven," replied Manfred, "does not send Heralds to question thetitle of a lawful Prince. I doubt whether it even notifies its willthrough Friars - but that is your affair, not mine. At present youknow my pleasure; and it is not a saucy Herald that shall save yourson, if you do not return with the Princess."

It was in vain for the holy man to reply. Manfred commanded him to beconducted to the postern-gate, and shut out from the castle. And heordered some of his attendants to carry Theodore to the top of theblack tower, and guard him strictly; scarce permitting the father andson to exchange a hasty embrace at parting. He then withdrew to thehall, and seating himself in princely state, ordered the Herald to beadmitted to his presence.

"Well! thou insolent!" said the Prince, "what wouldst thou with me?"

"I come," replied he, "to thee, Manfred, usurper of the principalityof Otranto, from the renowned and invincible Knight, the Knight of the Gigantic Sabre: in the name of his Lord, Frederic, Marquis of Vicenza, he demands the Lady Isabella, daughter of that Prince, whomthou hast basely and traitorously got into thy power, by bribing herfalse guardians during his absence; and he requires thee to resign theprincipality of Otranto, which thou hast usurped from the said Lord Frederic, the nearest of blood to the last rightful Lord, Alfonso the Good. If thou dost not instantly comply with these just demands, hedefies thee to single combat to the last extremity." And so sayingthe Herald cast down his warder.

"And where is this braggart who sends thee?" said Manfred. "At the distance of a league," said the Herald: "he comes to makegood his Lord's claim against thee, as he is a true knight, and thouan usurper and ravisher."

Injurious as this challenge was, Manfred reflected that it was not hisinterest to provoke the Marquis. He knew how well founded the claimof Frederic was; nor was this the first time he had heard of it. Frederic's ancestors had assumed the style of Princes of Otranto, fromthe death of Alfonso the Good without issue; but Manfred, his father,and grandfather, had been too powerful for the house of Vicenza todispossess them. Frederic, a martial and amorous young Prince, hadmarried a beautiful young lady, of whom he was enamoured, and who haddied in childbed of Isabella. Her death affected him so much that hehad taken the cross and gone to the Holy Land, where he was wounded inan engagement against the infidels, made prisoner, and reported to bedead. When the news reached Manfred's ears, he bribed the guardiansof the Lady Isabella to deliver her up to him as a bride for his son Conrad, by which alliance he had proposed to unite the claims of thetwo houses. This motive, on Conrad's death, had co-operated to makehim so suddenly resolve on espousing her himself; and the samereflection determined him now to endeavour at obtaining the consent of Frederic to this marriage. A like policy inspired him with thethought of inviting Frederic's champion into the castle, lest heshould be informed of Isabella's flight, which he strictly enjoinedhis domestics not to disclose to any of the Knight's retinue.

"Herald,"said Manfred, as soon as he had digested these reflections, "return to thy master, and tell him, ere we liquidate our differencesby the sword, Manfred would hold some converse with him. Bid himwelcome to my castle, where by my faith, as I am a true Knight, heshall have courteous reception, and full security for himself andfollowers. If we cannot adjust our quarrel by amicable means, I swearhe shall depart in safety, and shall have full satisfaction accordingto the laws of arms: So help me God and His holy Trinity!"

The Herald made three obeisances and retired.

During this interview Jerome's mind was agitated by a thousandcontrary passions. He trembled for the life of his son, and his firstthought was to persuade Isabella to return to the castle. Yet he wasscarce less alarmed at the thought of her union with Manfred. Hedreaded Hippolita's unbounded submission to the will of her Lord; andthough he did not doubt but he could alarm her piety not to consent toa divorce, if he could get access to her; yet should Manfred discoverthat the obstruction came from him, it might be equally fatal to Theodore. He was impatient to know whence came the Herald, who withso little management had questioned the title of Manfred: yet he didnot dare absent himself from the convent, lest Isabella should leaveit, and her flight be imputed to him. He returned disconsolately tothe monastery, uncertain on what conduct to resolve. A Monk, who methim in the porch and observed his melancholy air, said—"Alas! brother, is it then true that we have lost our excellent Princess Hippolita?"

The holy man started, and cried, "What meanest thou, brother? I comethis instant from the castle, and left her in perfect health."

"Martelli," replied the other Friar, "passed by the convent but aquarter of an hour ago on his way from the castle, and reported thather Highness was dead. All our brethren are gone to the chapel topray for her happy transit to a better life, and willed me to wait thyarrival. They know thy holy attachment to that good Lady, and areanxious for the affliction it will cause in thee - indeed we have allreason to weep; she was a mother to our house. But this life is but apilgrimage; we must not murmur - we shall all follow her! May our endbe like hers!"

"Good brother, thou dreamest," said Jerome. "I tell thee I come fromthe castle, and left the Princess well. Where is the Lady Isabella?"

"Poor Gentlewoman!" replied the Friar; "I told her the sad news, andoffered her spiritual comfort. I reminded her of the transitorycondition of mortality, and advised her to take the veil: I quotedthe example of the holy Princess Sanchia of Arragon."

"Thy zeal was laudable," said Jerome, impatiently; "but at present itwas unnecessary: Hippolita is well—at least I trust in the Lord sheis; I heard nothing to the contrary—yet, methinks, the Prince'searnestness - Well, brother, but where is the Lady Isabella?"

"I know not," said the Friar; "she wept much, and said she wouldretire to her chamber."

Jerome left his comrade abruptly, and hastened to the Princess, butshe was not in her chamber. He inquired of the domestics of theconvent, but could learn no news of her. He searched in vainthroughout the monastery and the church, and despatched messengersround the neighbourhood, to get intelligence if she had been seen; butto no purpose. Nothing could equal the good man's perplexity. Hejudged that Isabella, suspecting Manfred of having precipitated hiswife's death, had taken the alarm, and withdrawn herself to some moresecret place of concealment. This new flight would probably carry the Prince's fury to the height. The report of Hippolita's death, thoughit seemed almost incredible, increased his consternation; and though Isabella's escape bespoke her aversion of Manfred for a husband, Jerome could feel no comfort from it, while it endangered the life ofhis son. He determined to return to the castle, and made several ofhis brethren accompany him to attest his innocence to Manfred, and, ifnecessary, join their intercession with his for Theodore.

The Prince, in the meantime, had passed into the court, and orderedthe gates of the castle to be flung open for the reception of thestranger Knight and his train. In a few minutes the cavalcadearrived. First came two harbingers with wands. Next a herald,followed by two pages and two trumpets. Then a hundred foot-guards. These were attended by as many horse. After them fifty footmen,clothed in scarlet and black, the colours of the Knight. Then a ledhorse. Two heralds on each side of a gentleman on horseback bearing abanner with the arms of Vicenza and Otranto quarterly - a circumstancethat much offended Manfred - but he stifled his resentment. Two morepages. The Knight's confessor telling his beads. Fifty more footmenclad as before. Two Knights habited in complete armour, their beaversdown, comrades to the principal Knight. The squires of the two Knights, carrying their shields and devices. The Knight's own squire. A hundred gentlemen bearing an enormous sword, and seeming to faintunder the weight of it. The Knight himself on a chestnut steed, incomplete armour, his lance in the rest, his face entirely concealed byhis vizor, which was surmounted by a large plume of scarlet and blackfeathers. Fifty foot-guards with drums and trumpets closed theprocession, which wheeled off to the right and left to make room forthe principal Knight.

As soon as he approached the gate he stopped; and the heraldadvancing, read again the words of the challenge. Manfred's eyes werefixed on the gigantic sword, and he scarce seemed to attend to thecartel: but his attention was soon diverted by a tempest of wind thatrose behind him. He turned and beheld the Plumes of the enchantedhelmet agitated in the same extraordinary manner as before. Itrequired intrepidity like Manfred's not to sink under a concurrence ofcircumstances that seemed to announce his fate. Yet scorning in thepresence of strangers to betray the courage he had always manifested,he said boldly—

"Sir Knight, whoever thou art, I bid thee welcome. If thou art ofmortal mould, thy valour shall meet its equal: and if thou art a true Knight, thou wilt scorn to employ sorcery to carry thy point. Bethese omens from heaven or hell, Manfred trusts to the righteousnessof his cause and to the aid of St. Nicholas, who has ever protectedhis house. Alight, Sir Knight, and repose thyself. To-morrow thoushalt have a fair field, and heaven befriend the juster side!"

The Knight made no reply, but dismounting, was conducted by Manfred tothe great hall of the castle. As they traversed the court, the Knightstopped to gaze on the miraculous casque; and kneeling down, seemed topray inwardly for some minutes. Rising, he made a sign to the Princeto lead on. As soon as they entered the hall, Manfred proposed to thestranger to disarm, but the Knight shook his head in token of refusal.

"Sir Knight," said Manfred, "this is not courteous, but by my goodfaith I will not cross thee, nor shalt thou have cause to complain ofthe Prince of Otranto. No treachery is designed on my part; I hopenone is intended on thine; here take my gage" (giving him his ring) "your friends and you shall enjoy the laws of hospitality. Rest hereuntil refreshments are brought. I will but give orders for theaccommodation of your train, and return to you." The three Knightsbowed as accepting his courtesy. Manfred directed the stranger'sretinue to be conducted to an adjacent hospital, founded by the Princess Hippolita for the reception of pilgrims. As they made thecircuit of the court to return towards the gate, the gigantic swordburst from the supporters, and falling to the ground opposite to thehelmet, remained immovable. Manfred, almost hardened to preternaturalappearances, surmounted the shock of this new prodigy; and returningto the hall, where by this time the feast was ready, he invited hissilent guests to take their places. Manfred, however ill his heartwas at ease, endeavoured to inspire the company with mirth. He putseveral questions to them, but was answered only by signs. Theyraised their vizors but sufficiently to feed themselves, and that sparingly.

"Sirs" said the Prince, "ye are the first guests I ever treated withinthese walls who scorned to hold any intercourse with me: nor has itoft been customary, I ween, for princes to hazard their state anddignity against strangers and mutes. You say you come in the name of Frederic of Vicenza; I have ever heard that he was a gallant andcourteous Knight; nor would he, I am bold to say, think it beneath himto mix in social converse with a Prince that is his equal, and notunknown by deeds in arms. Still ye are silent - well! be it as it may— by the laws of hospitality and chivalry ye are masters under thisroof: ye shall do your pleasure. But come, give me a goblet of wine;ye will not refuse to pledge me to the healths of your fair mistresses."

The principal Knight sighed and crossed himself, and was rising fromthe board.

"Sir Knight," said Manfred, "what I said was but in sport. I shallconstrain you in nothing: use your good liking. Since mirth is notyour mood, let us be sad. Business may hit your fancies better. Letus withdraw, and hear if what I have to unfold may be better relishedthan the vain efforts I have made for your pastime."

Manfred then conducting the three Knights into an inner chamber, shutthe door, and inviting them to be seated, began thus, addressinghimself to the chief personage—

"You come, Sir Knight, as I understand, in the name of the Marquis of Vicenza, to re-demand the Lady Isabella, his daughter, who has beencontracted in the face of Holy Church to my son, by the consent of herlegal guardians; and to require me to resign my dominions to your Lord, who gives himself for the nearest of blood to Prince Alfonso,whose soul God rest! I shall speak to the latter article of yourdemands first. You must know, your Lord knows, that I enjoy theprincipality of Otranto from my father, Don Manuel, as he received itfrom his father, Don Ricardo. Alfonso, their predecessor, dyingchildless in the Holy Land, bequeathed his estates to my grandfather, Don Ricardo, in consideration of his faithful services." The stranger shook his head.

"Sir Knight," said Manfred, warmly, "Ricardo was a valiant and uprightman; he was a pious man; witness his munificent foundation of theadjoining church and two converts. He was peculiarly patronised by St. Nicholas - my grandfather was incapable - I say, Sir, Don Ricardowas incapable - excuse me, your interruption has disordered me. Ivenerate the memory of my grandfather. Well, Sirs, he held thisestate; he held it by his good sword and by the favour of St. Nicholas so did my father; and so, Sirs, will I, come what come will. But Frederic, your Lord, is nearest in blood. I have consented to put mytitle to the issue of the sword. Does that imply a vicious title? Imight have asked, where is Frederic your Lord? Report speaks him deadin captivity. You say, your actions say, he lives - I question it not—I might, Sirs, I might - but I do not. Other Princes would bid Frederic take his inheritance by force, if he can: they would notstake their dignity on a single combat: they would not submit it tothe decision of unknown mutes!—pardon me, gentlemen, I am too warm:but suppose yourselves in my situation: as ye are stout Knights,would it not move your choler to have your own and the honour of yourancestors called in question?"

"But to the point. Ye require me to deliver up the Lady Isabella.

Sirs, I must ask if ye are authorised to receive her?"

The Knight nodded.

"Receive her," continued Manfred; "well, you are authorised to receiveher, but, gentle Knight, may I ask if you have full powers?"

The Knight nodded.

"'Tis well," said Manfred; "then hear what I have to offer. Ye see,gentlemen, before you, the most unhappy of men!" (he began to weep); "afford me your compassion; I am entitled to it, indeed I am. Know, Ihave lost my only hope, my joy, the support of my house - Conrad diedyester morning."

The Knights discovered signs of surprise.

"Yes, Sirs, fate has disposed of my son. Isabella is at liberty."

"Do you then restore her?" cried the chief Knight, breaking silence.

"Afford me your patience," said Manfred. "I rejoice to find, by thistestimony of your goodwill, that this matter may be adjusted withoutblood. It is no interest of mine dictates what little I have fartherto say. Ye behold in me a man disgusted with the world: the loss ofmy son has weaned me from earthly cares. Power and greatness have nolonger any charms in my eyes. I wished to transmit the sceptre I hadreceived from my ancestors with honour to my son - but that is over! Life itself is so indifferent to me, that I accepted your defiancewith joy. A good Knight cannot go to the grave with more satisfactionthan when falling in his vocation: whatever is the will of heaven, Isubmit; for alas! Sirs, I am a man of many sorrows. Manfred is noobject of envy, but no doubt you are acquainted with my story."

The Knight made signs of ignorance, and seemed curious to have Manfred proceed.

"Is it possible, Sirs," continued the Prince, "that my story should bea secret to you? Have you heard nothing relating to me and the Princess Hippolita?"

They shook their heads.

"No! Thus, then, Sirs, it is. You think me ambitious: ambition,alas! is composed of more rugged materials. If I were ambitious, Ishould not for so many years have been a prey to all the hell ofconscientious scruples. But I weary your patience: I will be brief. Know, then, that I have long been troubled in mind on my union withthe Princess Hippolita. Oh! Sirs, if ye were acquainted with thatexcellent woman! if ye knew that I adore her like a mistress, andcherish her as a friend -

but man was not born for perfect happiness! She shares my scruples, and with her consent I have brought thismatter before the church, for we are related within the forbiddendegrees. I expect every hour the definitive sentence that mustseparate us for ever - I am sure you feel for me - I see you do -pardon these tears!"

The Knights gazed on each other, wondering where this would end.

Manfred continued -"The death of my son betiding while my soul was under this anxiety, Ithought of nothing but resigning my dominions, and retiring for everfrom the sight of mankind. My only difficulty was to fix on asuccessor, who would be tender of my people, and to dispose of the Lady Isabella, who is dear to me as my own blood. I was willing torestore the line of Alfonso, even in his most distant kindred. Andthough, pardon me, I am satisfied it was his will that Ricardo'slineage should take place of his own relations; yet where was I tosearch for those relations? I knew of none but Frederic, your Lord;he was a captive to the infidels, or dead; and were he living, and athome, would he quit the flourishing State of Vicenza for theinconsiderable principality of Otranto? If he would not, could I bearthe thought of seeing a hard, unfeeling, Viceroy set over my poorfaithful people? for, Sirs, I love my people, and thank heaven ambeloved by them. But ye will ask whither tends this long discourse? Briefly, then, thus, Sirs. Heaven in your arrival seems to point outa remedy for these difficulties and my misfortunes. The Lady Isabellais at liberty; I shall soon be so. I would submit to anything for thegood of my people. Were it not the best, the only way to extinguishthe feuds between our families, if I was to take the Lady Isabella towife? You start. But though Hippolita's virtues will ever be dear tome, a Prince must not consider himself; he is born for his people." Aservant at that instant entering the chamber apprised Manfred that Jerome and several of his brethren demanded immediate access to him.

The Prince, provoked at this interruption, and fearing that the Friarwould discover to the strangers that Isabella had taken sanctuary, wasgoing to forbid Jerome's entrance. But recollecting that he wascertainly arrived to notify the Princess's return, Manfred began toexcuse himself to the Knights for leaving them for a few moments, butwas prevented by the arrival of the Friars. Manfred angrilyreprimanded them for their intrusion, and would have forced them backfrom the chamber; but Jerome was too much agitated to be repulsed. Hedeclared aloud the flight of Isabella, with protestations of his own innocence.

Manfred, distracted at the news, and not less at its coming to theknowledge of the strangers, uttered nothing but incoherent sentences,now upbraiding the Friar, now apologising to the Knights, earnest toknow what was become of Isabella, yet equally afraid of their knowing;impatient to pursue her, yet dreading to have them join in thepursuit. He offered to despatch messengers in quest of her, but thechief Knight, no longer keeping silence, reproached Manfred in bitterterms for his dark and ambiguous dealing, and demanded the cause of Isabella's first absence from the castle. Manfred, casting a sternlook at Jerome, implying a command of silence, pretended that on Conrad's death he had placed her in sanctuary until he could determinehow to dispose of her. Jerome, who trembled for his son's life, didnot dare contradict this falsehood, but one of his brethren, not underthe same anxiety, declared frankly that she had fled to their churchin the preceding night. The Prince in vain endeavoured to stop thisdiscovery, which overwhelmed him with shame and confusion. Theprincipal stranger, amazed at the contradictions he heard, and morethan half persuaded that Manfred had secreted the Princess,notwithstanding the concern he expressed at her flight, rushing to thedoor, said—

"Thou traitor Prince! Isabella shall be found."

Manfred endeavoured to hold him, but the other Knights assisting theircomrade, he broke from the Prince, and hastened into the court,demanding his attendants. Manfred, finding it vain to divert him fromthe pursuit, offered to accompany him and summoning his attendants,and taking Jerome and some of the Friars to guide them, they issuedfrom the castle; Manfred privately giving orders to have the Knight'scompany secured, while to the knight he affected to despatch amessenger to require their assistance.

The company had no sooner quitted the castle than Matilda, who feltherself deeply interested for the young peasant, since she had seenhim condemned to death in the hall, and whose thoughts had been takenup with concerting measures to save him, was informed by some of thefemale attendants that Manfred had despatched all his men various waysin pursuit of Isabella. He had in his hurry given this order ingeneral terms, not meaning to extend it to the guard he had set upon Theodore, but forgetting it. The domestics, officious to obey soperemptory a Prince, and urged by their own curiosity and love ofnovelty to join in any precipitate chase, had to a man left thecastle. Matilda disengaged herself from her women, stole up to theblack tower, and unbolting the door, presented herself to theastonished Theodore.

"Young man," said she, "though filial duty and womanly modesty condemnthe step I am taking, yet holy charity, surmounting all other ties,justifies this act. Fly; the doors of thy prison are open: my fatherand his domestics are absent; but they may soon return. Be gone insafety; and may the angels of heaven direct thy course!"

"Thou art surely one of those angels!" said the enraptured Theodore: "none but a blessed saint could speak, could act - could look - likethee. May I not know the name of my divine protectress? Methoughtthou namedst thy father. Is it possible? Can Manfred's blood feelholy pity! Lovely Lady, thou answerest not. But how art thou herethyself? Why dost thou neglect thy own safety, and waste a thought ona wretch like Theodore? Let us fly together: the life thou bestowestshall be dedicated to thy defence."

"Alas! thou mistakest," said Matilda, signing: "I am Manfred'sdaughter, but no dangers await me."

"Amazement!" said Theodore; "but last night I blessed myself foryielding thee the service thy gracious compassion so charitably returns me now."

"Still thou art in an error," said the Princess; "but this is no timefor explanation. Fly, virtuous youth, while it is in my power to savethee: should my father return, thou and I both should indeed havecause to tremble."

"How!" said Theodore; "thinkest thou, charming maid, that I willaccept of life at the hazard of aught calamitous to thee? Better Iendured a thousand deaths."

"I run no risk," said Matilda, "but by thy delay. Depart; it cannotbe known that I have assisted thy flight."

"Swear by the saints above," said Theodore, "that thou canst not besuspected; else here I vow to await whatever can befall me."

"Oh! thou art too generous," said Matilda; "but rest assured that nosuspicion can alight on me."

"Give me thy beauteous hand in token that thou dost not deceive me,"said Theodore; "and let me bathe it with the warm tears of gratitude."

"Forbear!" said the Princess; "this must not be."

"Alas!" said Theodore, "I have never known but calamity until thishour - perhaps shall never know other fortune again: suffer the chaste raptures of holy gratitude: 'tis my soul would print itseffusions on thy hand."

"Forbear, and be gone," said Matilda. "How would Isabella approve ofseeing thee at my feet?"

"Who is Isabella?" said the young man with surprise.

"Ah, me! I fear," said the Princess, "I am serving a deceitful one.

Hast thou forgot thy curiosity this morning?"

"Thy looks, thy actions, all thy beauteous self seem an emanation ofdivinity," said Theodore; "but thy words are dark and mysterious. Speak, Lady; speak to thy servant's comprehension."

"Thou understandest but too well!" said Matilda; "but once more Icommand thee to be gone: thy blood, which I may preserve, will be onmy head, if I waste the time in vain discourse."

"I go, Lady," said Theodore, "because it is thy will, and because Iwould not bring the grey hairs of my father with sorrow to the grave. Say but, adored Lady, that I have thy gentle pity."

"Stay," said Matilda; "I will conduct thee to the subterraneous vaultby which Isabella escaped; it will lead thee to the church of St. Nicholas, where thou mayst take sanctuary."

"What!" said Theodore, "was it another, and not thy lovely self that Iassisted to find the subterraneous passage?"

"It was," said Matilda; "but ask no more; I tremble to see thee stillabide here; fly to the sanctuary."

"To sanctuary," said Theodore; "no, Princess; sanctuaries are forhelpless damsels, or for criminals. Theodore's soul is free fromguilt, nor will wear the appearance of it. Give me a sword, Lady, andthy father shall learn that Theodore scorns an ignominious flight."

"Rash youth!" said Matilda; "thou wouldst not dare to lift thypresumptuous arm against the Prince of Otranto?"

"Not against thy father; indeed, I dare not," said Theodore. "Excuseme, Lady; I had forgotten. But could I gaze on thee, and rememberthou art sprung from the tyrant Manfred! But he is thy father, andfrom this moment my injuries are buried in oblivion."

A deep and hollow groan, which seemed to come from above, startled the Princess and Theodore.

"Good heaven! we are overheard!" said the Princess. They listened;but perceiving no further noise, they both concluded it the effect ofpent-up vapours. And the Princess, preceding Theodore softly, carriedhim to her father's armoury, where, equipping him with a completesuit, he was conducted by Matilda to the postern-gate.

"Avoid the town," said the Princess, "and all the western side of thecastle. 'Tis there the search must be making by Manfred and thestrangers; but hie thee to the opposite quarter. Yonder behind thatforest to the east is a chain of rocks, hollowed into a labyrinth ofcaverns that reach to the sea coast. There thou mayst lie concealed,till thou canst make signs to some vessel to put on shore, and takethee off. Go! heaven be thy guide! - and sometimes in thy prayers remember— Matilda!"

Theodore flung himself at her feet, and seizing her lily hand, whichwith struggles she suffered him to kiss, he vowed on the earliestopportunity to get himself knighted, and fervently entreated herpermission to swear himself eternally her knight. Ere the Princesscould reply, a clap of thunder was suddenly heard that shook thebattlements. Theodore, regardless of the tempest, would have urgedhis suit: but the Princess, dismayed, retreated hastily into thecastle, and commanded the youth to be gone with an air that would notbe disobeyed. He sighed, and retired, but with eyes fixed on thegate, until Matilda, closing it, put an end to an interview, in whichthe hearts of both had drunk so deeply of a passion, which both nowtasted for the first time.

Theodore went pensively to the convent, to acquaint his father withhis deliverance. There he learned the absence of Jerome, and thepursuit that was making after the Lady Isabella, with some particularsof whose story he now first became acquainted. The generous gallantryof his nature prompted him to wish to assist her; but the Monks couldlend him no lights to guess at the route she had taken. He was nottempted to wander far in search of her, for the idea of Matilda hadimprinted itself so strongly on his heart, that he could not bear toabsent himself at much distance from her abode. The tenderness Jeromehad expressed for him concurred to confirm this reluctance; and heeven persuaded himself that filial affection was the chief cause ofhis hovering between the castle and monastery.

Until Jerome should return at night, Theodore at length determined torepair to the forest that Matilda had pointed out to him. Arrivingthere, he sought the gloomiest shades, as best suited to the pleasingmelancholy that reigned in his mind. In this mood he roved insensiblyto the caves which had formerly served as a retreat to hermits, andwere now reported round the country to be haunted by evil spirits. Herecollected to have heard this tradition; and being of a brave andadventurous disposition, he willingly indulged his curiosity inexploring the secret recesses of this labyrinth. He had notpenetrated far before he thought he heard the steps of some person whoseemed to retreat before him.

Theodore, though firmly grounded in all our holy faith enjoins to bebelieved, had no apprehension that good men were abandoned withoutcause to the malice of the powers of darkness. He thought the placemore likely to be infested by robbers than by those infernal agentswho are reported to molest and bewilder travellers. He had longburned with impatience to approve his valour. Drawing his sabre, hemarched sedately onwards, still directing his steps as the imperfectrustling sound before him led the way. The armour he wore was a likeindication to the person who avoided him. Theodore, now convincedthat he was not mistaken, redoubled his pace, and evidently gained onthe person that fled, whose haste increasing, Theodore came up just asa woman fell breathless before him. He hasted to raise her, but herterror was so great that he apprehended she would faint in his arms. He used every gentle word to dispel her alarms, and assured her thatfar from injuring, he would defend her at the peril of his life. The Lady recovering her spirits from his courteous demeanour, and gazingon her protector, said—

"Sure, I have heard that voice before!"

"Not to my knowledge," replied Theodore; "unless, as I conjecture,thou art the Lady Isabella."

"Merciful heaven!" cried she. "Thou art not sent in quest of me, artthou?" And saying those words, she threw herself at his feet, andbesought him not to deliver her up to Manfred.

"To Manfred!" cried Theodore—"no, Lady; I have once alreadydelivered thee from his tyranny, and it shall fare hard with me now,but I will place thee out of the reach of his daring."

"Is it possible," said she, "that thou shouldst be the generousunknown whom I met last night in the vault of the castle? Sure thouart not a mortal, but my guardian angel. On my knees, let me thank —"

"Hold! gentle Princess," said Theodore, "nor demean thyself before apoor and friendless young man. If heaven has selected me for thydeliverer, it will accomplish its work, and strengthen my arm in thycause. But come, Lady, we are too near the mouth of the cavern; letus seek its inmost recesses. I can have no tranquillity till I haveplaced thee beyond the reach of danger."

"Alas! what mean you, sir?" said she. "Though all your actions arenoble, though your sentiments speak the purity of your soul, is itfitting that I should accompany you alone into these perplexedretreats? Should we be found together, what would a censorious worldthink of my conduct?"

"I respect your virtuous delicacy," said Theodore; "nor do you harboura suspicion that wounds my honour. I meant to conduct you into themost private cavity of these rocks, and then at the hazard of my lifeto guard their entrance against every living thing. Besides, Lady,"continued he, drawing a deep sigh, "beauteous and all perfect as yourform is, and though my wishes are not guiltless of aspiring, know, mysoul is dedicated to another; and although—" A sudden noiseprevented Theodore from proceeding. They soon distinguished these sounds—

"Isabella! what, ho! Isabella!" The trembling Princess relapsed intoher former agony of fear. Theodore endeavoured to encourage her, butin vain. He assured her he would die rather than suffer her to returnunder Manfred's power; and begging her to remain concealed, he wentforth to prevent the person in search of her from approaching.

At the mouth of the cavern he found an armed Knight, discoursing witha peasant, who assured him he had seen a lady enter the passes of therock. The Knight was preparing to seek her, when Theodore, placinghimself in his way, with his sword drawn, sternly forbad him at hisperil to advance.

"And who art thou, who darest to cross my way?" said the Knight, haughtily.

"One who does not dare more than he will perform," said Theodore.

"I seek the Lady Isabella," said the Knight, "and understand she hastaken refuge among these rocks. Impede me not, or thou wilt repenthaving provoked my resentment."

"Thy purpose is as odious as thy resentment is contemptible," said

Theodore. "Return whence thou camest, or we shall soon know whoseresentment is most terrible."

The stranger, who was the principal Knight that had arrived from the Marquis of Vicenza, had galloped from Manfred as he was busied ingetting information of the Princess, and giving various orders toprevent her falling into the power of the three Knights. Their chiefhad suspected Manfred of being privy to the Princess's absconding, andthis insult from a man, who he concluded was stationed by that Princeto secrete her, confirming his suspicions, he made no reply, butdischarging a blow with his sabre at Theodore, would soon have removedall obstruction, if Theodore, who took him for one of Manfred'scaptains, and who had no sooner given the provocation than prepared tosupport it, had not received the stroke on his shield. The valourthat had so long been smothered in his breast broke forth at once; herushed impetuously on the Knight, whose pride and wrath were not lesspowerful incentives to hardy deeds. The combat was furious, but notlong. Theodore wounded the Knight in three several places, and atlast disarmed him as he fainted by the loss of blood.

The peasant, who had fled on the first onset, had given the alarm tosome of Manfred's domestics, who, by his orders, were dispersedthrough the forest in pursuit of Isabella. They came up as the Knightfell, whom they soon discovered to be the noble stranger. Theodore,notwithstanding his hatred to Manfred, could not behold the victory hehad gained without emotions of pity and generosity. But he was moretouched when he learned the quality of his adversary, and was informedthat he was no retainer, but an enemy, of Manfred. He assisted theservants of the latter in disarming the Knight, and in endeavouring tostanch the blood that flowed from his wounds. The Knight recoveringhis speech, said, in a faint and faltering voice—

"Generous foe, we have both been in an error. I took thee for aninstrument of the tyrant; I perceive thou hast made the like mistake.

It is too late for excuses. I faint. If Isabella is at hand— callher— I have important secrets to—"

"He is dying!" said one of the attendants; "has nobody a crucifixabout them? Andrea, do thou pray over him."

"Fetch some water," said Theodore, "and pour it down his throat, while I hasten to the Princess."

Saying this, he flew to Isabella, and in few words told her modestlythat he had been so unfortunate by mistake as to wound a gentlemanfrom her father's court, who wished, ere he died, to impart somethingof consequence to her.

The Princess, who had been transported at hearing the voice of Theodore, as he called to her to come forth, was astonished at whatshe heard. Suffering herself to be conducted by Theodore, the newproof of whose valour recalled her dispersed spirits, she came wherethe bleeding Knight lay speechless on the ground. But her fearsreturned when she beheld the domestics of Manfred. She would againhave fled if Theodore had not made her observe that they were unarmed,and had not threatened them with instant death if they should dare toseize the Princess.

The stranger, opening his eyes, and beholding a woman, said, "Art thou—pray tell me truly—art thou Isabella of Vicenza?"

"I am," said she: "good heaven restore thee!"

"Then thou - then thou" —said the Knight, struggling for utterance —"seest - thy father. Give me one—"

"Oh! amazement! horror! what do I hear! what do I see!" cried Isabella. "My father! You my father! How came you here, Sir? Forheaven's sake, speak! Oh! run for help, or he will expire!"

"'Tis most true," said the wounded Knight, exerting all his force; "Iam Frederic thy father. Yes, I came to deliver thee. It will not be. Give me a parting kiss, and take— "

"Sir," said Theodore, "do not exhaust yourself; suffer us to conveyyou to the castle."

"To the castle!" said Isabella. "Is there no help nearer than thecastle? Would you expose my father to the tyrant? If he goesthither, I dare not accompany him; and yet, can I leave him!"

"My child," said Frederic, "it matters not for me whither I amcarried. A few minutes will place me beyond danger; but while I haveeyes to dote on thee, forsake me not, dear Isabella! This brave Knight - I know not who he is - will protect thy innocence. Sir, youwill not abandon my child, will you?"

Theodore, shedding tears over his victim, and vowing to guard the Princess at the expense of his life, persuaded Frederic to sufferhimself to be conducted to the castle. They placed him on a horsebelonging to one of the domestics, after binding up his wounds as wellas they were able. Theodore marched by his side; and the afflicted Isabella, who could not bear to quit him, followed mournfully behind.

CHAPTER - IV

The sorrowful troop no sooner arrived at the castle, than they weremet by Hippolita and Matilda, whom Isabella had sent one of thedomestics before to advertise of their approach. The ladies causing Frederic to be conveyed into the nearest chamber, retired, while thesurgeons examined his wounds. Matilda blushed at seeing Theodore and Isabella together; but endeavoured to conceal it by embracing thelatter, and condoling with her on her father's mischance. Thesurgeons soon came to acquaint Hippolita that none of the Marquis'swounds were dangerous; and that he was desirous of seeing his daughterand the Princesses.

Theodore, under pretence of expressing his joy at being freed from hisapprehensions of the combat being fatal to Frederic, could not resistthe impulse of following Matilda. Her eyes were so often cast down onmeeting his, that Isabella, who regarded Theodore as attentively as hegazed on Matilda, soon divined who the object was that he had told herin the cave engaged his affections. While this mute scene passed, Hippolita demanded of Frederic the cause of his having taken thatmysterious course for reclaiming his daughter; and threw in variousapologies to excuse her Lord for the match contracted between theirchildren.

Frederic, however incensed against Manfred, was not insensible to thecourtesy and benevolence of Hippolita: but he was still more struckwith the lovely form of Matilda. Wishing to detain them by hisbedside, he informed Hippolita of his story. He told her that, whileprisoner to the infidels, he had dreamed that his daughter, of whom hehad learned no news since his captivity, was detained in a castle,where she was in danger of the most dreadful misfortunes: and that ifhe obtained his liberty, and repaired to a wood near Joppa, he wouldlearn more. Alarmed at this dream, and incapable of obeying thedirection given by it, his chains became more grievous than ever. Butwhile his thoughts were occupied on the means of obtaining hisliberty, he received the agreeable news that the confederate Princeswho were warring in Palestine had paid his ransom. He instantly setout for the wood that had been marked in his dream.

For three days he and his attendants had wandered in the forestwithout seeing a human form: but on the evening of the third theycame to a cell, in which they found a venerable hermit in the agoniesof death. Applying rich cordials, they brought the fainting man tohis speech.

"My sons," said he, "I am bounden to your charity— but it is in vain—I am going to my eternal rest— yet I die with the satisfaction ofperforming the will of heaven. When first I repaired to thissolitude, after seeing my country become a prey to unbelievers - it isalas! above fifty years since I was witness to that dreadful scene! St. Nicholas appeared to me, and revealed a secret, which he bade menever disclose to mortal man, but on my death-bed. This is thattremendous hour, and ye are no doubt the chosen warriors to whom I wasordered to reveal my trust. As soon as ye have done the last officesto this wretched corse, dig under the seventh tree on the left hand ofthis poor cave, and your pains will - Oh! good heaven receive mysoul!" With those words the devout man breathed his last.

"By break of day," continued Frederic, "when we had committed the holyrelics to earth, we dug according to direction. But what was ourastonishment when about the depth of six feet we discovered anenormous sabre - the very weapon yonder in the court. On the blade,which was then partly out of the scabbard, though since closed by ourefforts in removing it, were written the following lines— no; excuseme, Madam," added the Marquis, turning to Hippolita; "if I forbear torepeat them: I respect your sex and rank, and would not be guilty ofoffending your ear with sounds injurious to aught that is dear to you."

He paused. Hippolita trembled. She did not doubt but Frederic wasdestined by heaven to accomplish the fate that seemed to threaten herhouse. Looking with anxious fondness at Matilda, a silent tear stoledown her cheek: but recollecting herself, she said—

"Proceed, my Lord; heaven does nothing in vain; mortals must receiveits divine behests with lowliness and submission. It is our part todeprecate its wrath, or bow to its decrees. Repeat the sentence, my Lord; we listen resigned."

Frederic was grieved that he had proceeded so far. The dignity andpatient firmness of Hippolita penetrated him with respect, and thetender silent affection with which the Princess and her daughterregarded each other, melted him almost to tears. Yet apprehensivethat his forbearance to obey would be more alarming, he repeated in afaltering and low voice the following lines:

"Where'er a casque that suits this sword is found,

With perils is thy daughter compass'd round;

Alfonso's blood alone can save the maid,

And quiet a long restless Prince's shade."

"What is there in these lines," said Theodore impatiently, "thataffects these Princesses? Why were they to be shocked by a mysteriousdelicacy, that has so little foundation?"

"Your words are rude, young man," said the Marquis; "and thoughfortune has favoured you once— "

"My honoured Lord," said Isabella, who resented Theodore's warmth,which she perceived was dictated by his sentiments for Matilda,

"discompose not yourself for the glosing of a peasant's son: heforgets the reverence he owes you; but he is not accustomed—"

Hippolita, concerned at the heat that had arisen, checked Theodore forhis boldness, but with an air acknowledging his zeal; and changing theconversation, demanded of Frederic where he had left her Lord? As the Marquis was going to reply, they heard a noise without, and rising toinquire the cause, Manfred, Jerome, and part of the troop, who had metan imperfect rumour of what had happened, entered the chamber.

Manfred advanced hastily towards Frederic's bed to condole with him onhis misfortune, and to learn the circumstances of the combat, whenstarting in an agony of terror and amazement, he cried —

"Ha! what art thou? thou dreadful spectre! is my hour come?"

"My dearest, gracious Lord," cried Hippolita, clasping him in herarms, "what is it you see! Why do you fix your eye-balls thus?"

"What!" cried Manfred breathless; "dost thou see nothing, Hippolita? Is this ghastly phantom sent to me alone—to rue, who did not—"

"For mercy's sweetest self, my Lord," said Hippolita, "resume yoursoul, command your reason. There is none here, but us, your friends."

"What, is not that Alfonso?" cried Manfred. "Dost thou not see him?can it be my brain's delirium?"

"This! my Lord," said Hippolita; "this is Theodore, the youth who hasbeen so unfortunate."

"Theodore!" said Manfred mournfully, and striking his forehead; "Theodore or a phantom, he has unhinged the soul of Manfred. But howcomes he here? and how comes he in armour?"

"I believe he went in search of Isabella," said Hippolita.

"Of Isabella!" said Manfred, relapsing into rage; "yes, yes, that isnot doubtful—. But how did he escape from durance in which I lefthim? Was it Isabella, or this hypocritical old Friar, that procuredhis enlargement?"

"And would a parent be criminal, my Lord," said Theodore, "if hemeditated the deliverance of his child?"

Jerome, amazed to hear himself in a manner accused by his son, andwithout foundation, knew not what to think. He could not comprehendhow Theodore had escaped, how he came to be armed, and to encounter

Frederic. Still he would not venture to ask any questions that mighttend to inflame Manfred's wrath against his son. Jerome's silenceconvinced Manfred that he had contrived Theodore's release.

"And is it thus, thou ungrateful old man," said the Prince, addressinghimself to the Friar, "that thou repayest mine and Hippolita'sbounties? And not content with traversing my heart's nearest wishes,thou armest thy bastard, and bringest him into my own castle to insult me!"

"My Lord," said Theodore, "you wrong my father: neither he nor I arecapable of harbouring a thought against your peace. Is it insolencethus to surrender myself to your Highness's pleasure?" added he,laying his sword respectfully at Manfred's feet. "Behold my bosom;strike, my Lord, if you suspect that a disloyal thought is lodgedthere. There is not a sentiment engraven on my heart that does notvenerate you and yours."

The grace and fervour with which Theodore uttered these wordsinterested every person present in his favour. Even Manfred wastouched—yet still possessed with his resemblance to Alfonso, hisadmiration was dashed with secret horror.

"Rise," said he; "thy life is not my present purpose. But tell me thyhistory, and how thou camest connected with this old traitor here."

"My Lord," said Jerome eagerly.

"Peace! impostor!" said Manfred; "I will not have him prompted."

"My Lord," said Theodore, "I want no assistance; my story is verybrief. I was carried at five years of age to Algiers with my mother,who had been taken by corsairs from the coast of Sicily. She died ofgrief in less than a twelvemonth;" the tears gushed from Jerome'seyes, on whose countenance a thousand anxious passions stoodexpressed. "Before she died," continued Theodore, "she bound awriting about my arm under my garments, which told me I was the son ofthe Count Falconara."

"It is most true," said Jerome; "I am that wretched father."

"Again I enjoin thee silence," said Manfred: "proceed."

"I remained in slavery," said Theodore, "until within these two years,when attending on my master in his cruises, I was delivered by a Christian vessel, which overpowered the pirate; and discovering myselfto the captain, he generously put me on shore in Sicily; but alas!instead of finding a father, I learned that his estate, which wassituated on the coast, had, during his absence, been laid waste by the Rover who had carried my mother and me into captivity: that hiscastle had been burnt to the ground, and that my father on his returnhad sold what remained, and was retired into religion in the kingdomof Naples, but where no man could inform me. Destitute andfriendless, hopeless almost of attaining the transport of a parent'sembrace, I took the first opportunity of setting sail for Naples, fromwhence, within these six days, I wandered into this province, stillsupporting myself by the labour of my hands; nor until yester-morn did I believe that heaven had reserved any lot for me but peace of mindand contented poverty. This, my Lord, is Theodore's story. I amblessed beyond my hope in finding a father; I am unfortunate beyond mydesert in having incurred your Highness's displeasure."

He ceased. A murmur of approbation gently arose from the audience.

"This is not all," said Frederic; "I am bound in honour to add what hesuppresses. Though he is modest, I must be generous; he is one of thebravest youths on Christian ground. He is warm too; and from theshort knowledge I have of him, I will pledge myself for his veracity:if what he reports of himself were not true, he would not utter it -and for me, youth, I honour a frankness which becomes thy birth; butnow, and thou didst offend me: yet the noble blood which flows in thyveins, may well be allowed to boil out, when it has so recently traceditself to its source. Come, my Lord," (turning to Manfred), "if I canpardon him, surely you may; it is not the youth's fault, if you tookhim for a spectre."

This bitter taunt galled the soul of Manfred.

"If beings from another world," replied he haughtily, "have power toimpress my mind with awe, it is more than living man can do; nor coulda stripling's arm."

"My Lord," interrupted Hippolita, "your guest has occasion for repose:shall we not leave him to his rest?" Saying this, and taking Manfredby the hand, she took leave of Frederic, and led the company forth.

The Prince, not sorry to quit a conversation which recalled to mindthe discovery he had made of his most secret sensations, sufferedhimself to be conducted to his own apartment, after permitting Theodore, though under engagement to return to the castle on themorrow (a condition the young man gladly accepted), to retire with hisfather to the convent. Matilda and Isabella were too much occupiedwith their own reflections, and too little content with each other, towish for farther converse that night. They separated each to herchamber, with more expressions of ceremony and fewer of affection thouhad passed between them since their childhood.

If they parted with small cordiality, they did but meet with greaterimpatience, as soon as the sun was risen. Their minds were in asituation that excluded sleep, and each recollected a thousandquestions which she wished she had put to the other overnight. Matilda reflected that Isabella had been twice delivered by Theodorein very critical situations, which she could not believe accidental. His eyes, it was true, had been fixed on her in Frederic's chamber;but that might have been to disguise his passion for Isabella from thefathers of both. It were better to clear this up. She wished to knowthe truth, lest she should wrong her friend by entertaining a passionfor Isabella's lover. Thus jealousy prompted, and at the same timeborrowed an excuse from friendship to justify its curiosity.

Isabella, not less restless, had better foundation for her suspicions. Both Theodore's tongue and eyes had told her his heart was engaged; itwas true - yet, perhaps, Matilda might not correspond to his passion;she had ever appeared insensible to love: all her thoughts were seton heaven.

"Why did I dissuade her?" said Isabella to herself; "I am punished formy generosity; but when did they meet? where? It cannot be; I havedeceived myself; perhaps last night was the first time they everbeheld each other; it must be some other object that has prepossessedhis affections - if it is, I am not so unhappy as I thought; if it isnot my friend Matilda - how! Can I stoop to wish for the affection ofa man, who rudely and unnecessarily acquainted me with hisindifference? and that at the very moment in which common courtesydemanded at least expressions of civility. I will go to my dear Matilda, who will confirm me in this becoming pride. Man is false - Iwill advise with her on taking the veil: she will rejoice to find mein this disposition; and I will acquaint her that I no longer opposeher inclination for the cloister."

In this frame of mind, and determined to open her heart entirely to Matilda, she went to that Princess's chamber, whom she found alreadydressed, and leaning pensively on her arm. This attitude, socorrespondent to what she felt herself, revived Isabella's suspicions,and destroyed the confidence she had purposed to place in her friend. They blushed at meeting, and were too much novices to disguise theirsensations with address. After some unmeaning questions and replies, Matilda demanded of Isabella the cause of her flight? The latter, whohad almost forgotten Manfred's passion, so entirely was she occupiedby her own, concluding that Matilda referred to her last escape fromthe convent, which had occasioned the events of the preceding evening,replied—

"Martelli brought word to the convent that your mother was dead."

"Oh!"said Matilda, interrupting her, "Bianca has explained thatmistake to me: on seeing me faint, she cried out, 'The Princess isdead!' and Martelli, who had come for the usual dole to the castle—

"And what made you faint?" said Isabella, indifferent to the rest.

Matilda blushed and stammered—

"My father - he was sitting in judgment on a criminal—"

"What criminal?" said Isabella eagerly.

"A young man," said Matilda; "I believe - "

"I think it was that young man that - "

"What, Theodore?" said Isabella.

"Yes," answered she; "I never saw him before; I do not know how he hadoffended my father, but as he has been of service to you, I am glad my Lord has pardoned him."

"Served me!" replied Isabella; "do you term it serving me, to wound myfather, and almost occasion his death? Though it is but sinceyesterday that I am blessed with knowing a parent, I hope Matilda doesnot think I am such a stranger to filial tenderness as not to resentthe boldness of that audacious youth, and that it is impossible for meever to feel any affection for one who dared to lift his arm againstthe author of my being. No, Matilda, my heart abhors him; and if youstill retain the friendship for me that you have vowed from yourinfancy, you will detest a man who has been on the point of making memiserable for ever."

Matilda held down her head and replied: "I hope my dearest Isabelladoes not doubt her Matilda's friendship: I never beheld that youthuntil yesterday; he is almost a stranger to me: but as the surgeonshave pronounced your father out of danger, you ought not to harbouruncharitable resentment against one, who I am persuaded did not knowthe Marquis was related to you."

"You plead his cause very pathetically," said Isabella, "consideringhe is so much a stranger to you! I am mistaken, or he returns your charity."

"What mean you?" said Matilda.

"Nothing," said Isabella, repenting that she had given Matilda a hintof Theodore's inclination for her. Then changing the discourse, sheasked Matilda what occasioned Manfred to take Theodore for a spectre?

"Bless me," said Matilda, "did not you observe his extreme resemblanceto the portrait of Alfonso in the gallery? I took notice of it to Bianca even before I saw him in armour; but with the helmet on, he isthe very image of that picture."

"I do not much observe pictures," said Isabella: "much less have Iexamined this young man so attentively as you seem to have done. Ah? Matilda, your heart is in danger, but let me warn you as a friend, hehas owned to me that he is in love; it cannot be with you, foryesterday was the first time you ever met—was it not?"

"Certainly," replied Matilda; "but why does my dearest Isabellaconclude from anything I have said, that" - she paused - thencontinuing: "he saw you first, and I am far from having the vanity tothink that my little portion of charms could engage a heart devoted toyou; may you be happy, Isabella, whatever is the fate of Matilda!"

"My lovely friend," said Isabella, whose heart was too honest toresist a kind expression, "it is you that Theodore admires; I saw it; I am persuaded of it; nor shall a thought of my own happiness sufferme to interfere with yours."

This frankness drew tears from the gentle Matilda; and jealousy thatfor a moment had raised a coolness between these amiable maidens soongave way to the natural sincerity and candour of their souls. Eachconfessed to the other the impression that Theodore had made on her;and this confidence was followed by a struggle of generosity, eachinsisting on yielding her claim to her friend. At length the dignityof Isabella's virtue reminding her of the preference which Theodorehad almost declared for her rival, made her determine to conquer herpassion, and cede the beloved object to her friend.

During this contest of amity, Hippolita entered her daughter's chamber.

"Madam," said she to Isabella, "you have so much tenderness for Matilda, and interest yourself so kindly in whatever affects ourwretched house, that I can have no secrets with my child which are notproper for you to hear."

The princesses were all attention and anxiety.

"Know then, Madam," continued Hippolita, "and you my dearest Matilda,that being convinced by all the events of these two last ominous days,that heaven purposes the sceptre of Otranto should pass from Manfred'shands into those of the Marquis Frederic, I have been perhaps inspiredwith the thought of averting our total destruction by the union of ourrival houses. With this view I have been proposing to Manfred, mylord, to tender this dear, dear child to Frederic, your father."

"Me to Lord Frederic!" cried Matilda; "good heavens! my graciousmother - and have you named it to my father?"

"I have," said Hippolita; "he listened benignly to my proposal, and isgone to break it to the Marquis."

"Ah! wretched princess!" cried Isabella; "what hast thou done! whatruin has thy inadvertent goodness been preparing for thyself, for me,and for Matilda!"

"Ruin from me to you and to my child!" said Hippolita "what can this mean?"

"Alas!"said Isabella,"the purity of your own heart prevents yourseeing the depravity of others. Manfred, your lord, that impious man—"

"Hold," said Hippolita; "you must not in my presence, young lady,mention Manfred with disrespect: he is my lord and husband, and—

"Will not long be so," said Isabella, "if his wicked purposes can becarried into execution."

"This language amazes me," said Hippolita. "Your feeling, Isabella,is warm; but until this hour I never knew it betray you intointemperance. What deed of Manfred authorises you to treat him as amurderer, an assassin?"

"Thou virtuous, and too credulous Princess!" replied Isabella; "it isnot thy life he aims at—it is to separate himself from thee! todivorce thee! to—"

"To divorce me!" "To divorce my mother!" cried Hippolita and Matildaat once.

"Yes," said Isabella; "and to complete his crime, he meditates—Icannot speak it!"

"What can surpass what thou hast already uttered?" said Matilda.

Hippolita was silent. Grief choked her speech; and the recollectionof Manfred's late ambiguous discourses confirmed what she heard.

"Excellent, dear lady! madam! mother!" cried Isabella, flingingherself at Hippolita's feet in a transport of passion; "trust me,believe me, I will die a thousand deaths sooner than consent to injureyou, than yield to so odious—oh!—"

"This is too much!" cried Hippolita: "What crimes does one crimesuggest! Rise, dear Isabella; I do not doubt your virtue. Oh! Matilda, this stroke is too heavy for thee! weep not, my child; andnot a murmur, I charge thee. Remember, he is thy father still!"

"But you are my mother too," said Matilda fervently; "and you arevirtuous, you are guiltless!—Oh! must not I, must not I complain?"

"You must not," said Hippolita - "come, all will yet be well. Manfred, in the agony for the loss of thy brother, knew not what hesaid; perhaps Isabella misunderstood him; his heart is good - and, mychild, thou knowest not all! There is a destiny hangs over us; thehand of

Providence is stretched out; oh! could I but save thee fromthe wreck! Yes," continued she in a firmer tone, "perhaps thesacrifice of myself may atone for all; I will go and offer myself tothis divorce - it boots not what becomes of me. I will withdraw intothe neighbouring monastery, and waste the remainder of life in prayersand tears for my child and— the Prince!"

"Thou art as much too good for this world," said Isabella, "as Manfredis execrable; but think not, lady, that thy weakness shall determinefor me. I swear, hear me all ye angels—"

"Stop, I adjure thee," cried Hippolita: "remember thou dost notdepend on thyself; thou hast a father."

"My father is too pious, too noble," interrupted Isabella, "to commandan impious deed. But should he command it; can a father enjoin acursed act? I was contracted to the son, can I wed the father? No,madam, no; force should not drag me to Manfred's hated bed. I loathehim, I abhor him: divine and human laws forbid - and my friend, mydearest Matilda! would I wound her tender soul by injuring her adoredmother? my own mother—I never have known another"—

"Oh! she is the mother of both!" cried Matilda: "can we, can we,

Isabella, adore her too much?"

"My lovely children," said the touched Hippolita, "your tendernessoverpowers me—but I must not give way to it. It is not ours to makeelection for ourselves: heaven, our fathers, and our husbands mustdecide for us. Have patience until you hear what Manfred and Frederichave determined. If the Marquis accepts Matilda's hand, I know shewill readily obey. Heaven may interpose and prevent the rest. Whatmeans my child?" continued she, seeing Matilda fall at her feet with aflood of speechless tears - "But no; answer me not, my daughter: Imust not hear a word against the pleasure of thy father."

"Oh! doubt not my obedience, my dreadful obedience to him and to you!"said Matilda. "But can I, most respected of women, can I experienceall this tenderness, this world of goodness, and conceal a thoughtfrom the best of mothers?"

"What art thou going to utter?" said Isabella trembling. "Recollectthyself, Matilda."

"No, Isabella," said the Princess, "I should not deserve thisincomparable parent, if the inmost recesses of my soul harboured athought without her permission—nay, I have offended her; I havesuffered a passion to enter my heart without her avowal —but here Idisclaim it; here I vow to heaven and her— "

"My child! my child;" said Hippolita, "what words are these! what newcalamities has fate in store for us! Thou, a passion? Thou, in thishour of destruction— "

"Oh! I see all my guilt!" said Matilda. "I abhor myself, if I cost mymother a pang. She is the dearest thing I have on earth—Oh! I willnever, never behold him more!"

"Isabella," said Hippolita, "thou art conscious to this unhappysecret, whatever it is. Speak!"

"What!" cried Matilda, "have I so forfeited my mother's love, that shewill not permit me even to speak my own guilt? oh! wretched, wretched Matilda!"

"Thou art too cruel," said Isabella to Hippolita: "canst thou beholdthis anguish of a virtuous mind, and not commiserate it?"

"Not pity my child!" said Hippolita, catching Matilda in her arms —"Oh! I know she is good, she is all virtue, all tenderness, and duty. I do forgive thee, my excellent, my only hope!"

The princesses then revealed to Hippolita their mutual inclination for Theodore, and the purpose of Isabella to resign him to Matilda. Hippolita blamed their imprudence, and showed them the improbabilitythat either father would consent to bestow his heiress on so poor aman, though nobly born. Some comfort it gave her to find theirpassion of so recent a date, and that Theodore had had but littlecause to suspect it in either. She strictly enjoined them to avoidall correspondence with him. This Matilda fervently promised: but Isabella, who flattered herself that she meant no more than to promotehis union with her friend, could not determine to avoid him; and madeno reply.

"I will go to the convent," said Hippolita, "and order new masses tobe said for a deliverance from these calamities."

"Oh! my mother," said Matilda, "you mean to quit us: you mean to takesanctuary, and to give my father an opportunity of pursuing his fatalintention. Alas! on my knees I supplicate you to forbear; will youleave me a prey to Frederic? I will follow you to the convent."

"Be at peace, my child," said Hippolita: "I will return instantly. Iwill never abandon thee, until I know it is the will of heaven, andfor thy benefit."

"Do not deceive me," said Matilda. "I will not marry Frederic untilthou commandest it. Alas! what will become of me?"

"Why that exclamation?" said Hippolita. "I have promised thee toreturn—"

"Ah! my mother," replied Matilda, "stay and save me from myself. Afrown from thee can do more than all my father's severity. I havegiven away my heart, and you alone can make me recall it."

"No more," said Hippolita; "thou must not relapse, Matilda."

"I can quit Theodore," said she, "but must I wed another? let meattend thee to the altar, and shut myself from the world for ever."

"Thy fate depends on thy father," said Hippolita; "I have ill-bestowedmy tenderness, if it has taught thee to revere aught beyond him. Adieu! my child: I go to pray for thee."

Hippolita's real purpose was to demand of Jerome, whether inconscience she might not consent to the divorce. She had oft urged

Manfred to resign the principality, which the delicacy of herconscience rendered an hourly burthen to her. These scruplesconcurred to make the separation from her husband appear less dreadfulto her than it would have seemed in any other situation.

Jerome, at quitting the castle overnight, had questioned Theodoreseverely why he had accused him to Manfred of being privy to hisescape. Theodore owned it had been with design to prevent Manfred'ssuspicion from alighting on Matilda; and added, the holiness of Jerome's life and character secured him from the tyrant's wrath.

Jerome was heartily grieved to discover his son's inclination for thatprincess; and leaving him to his rest, promised in the morning toacquaint him with important reasons for conquering his passion.

Theodore, like Isabella, was too recently acquainted with parentalauthority to submit to its decisions against the impulse of his heart. He had little curiosity to learn the Friar's reasons, and lessdisposition to obey them. The lovely Matilda had made strongerimpressions on him than filial affection. All night he pleasedhimself with visions of love; and it was not till late after themorning-office, that he recollected the Friar's commands to attend himat Alfonso's tomb.

"Young man," said Jerome, when he saw him, "this tardiness does notplease me. Have a father's commands already so little weight?"

Theodore made awkward excuses, and attributed his delay to havingoverslept himself.

"And on whom were thy dreams employed?" said the Friar sternly. Hisson blushed. "Come, come," resumed the Friar, "inconsiderate youth,this must not be; eradicate this guilty passion from thy breast—

"Guilty passion!" cried Theodore: "Can guilt dwell with innocentbeauty and virtuous modesty?"

"It is sinful," replied the Friar, "to cherish those whom heaven hasdoomed to destruction. A tyrant's race must be swept from the earthto the third and fourth generation."

"Will heaven visit the innocent for the crimes of the guilty?" said Theodore. "The fair Matilda has virtues enough—"

"To undo thee:" interrupted Jerome. "Hast thou so soon forgotten thattwice the savage Manfred has pronounced thy sentence?"

"Nor have I forgotten, sir," said Theodore, "that the charity of hisdaughter delivered me from his power. I can forget injuries, butnever benefits."

"The injuries thou hast received from Manfred's race," said the Friar, "are beyond what thou canst conceive. Reply not, but view this holyimage! Beneath this marble monument rest the ashes of the good

Alfonso; a prince adorned with every virtue: the father of hispeople! the delight of mankind! Kneel, headstrong boy, and list,while a father unfolds a tale of horror that will expel everysentiment from thy soul, but sensations of sacred vengeance—Alfonso!much injured prince! let thy unsatisfied shade sit awful on thetroubled air, while these trembling lips—Ha! who comes there?—"

"The most wretched of women!" said Hippolita, entering the choir.

"Good Father, art thou at leisure?—but why this kneeling youth? whatmeans the horror imprinted on each countenance? why at this venerabletomb - alas! hast thou seen aught?"

"We were pouring forth our orisons to heaven," replied the Friar, withsome confusion,"to put an end to the woes of this deplorableprovince. Join with us, Lady! thy spotless soul may obtain anexemption from the judgments which the portents of these days but toospeakingly denounce against thy house."

"I pray fervently to heaven to divert them," said the pious Princess.

"Thou knowest it has been the occupation of my life to wrest ablessing for my Lord and my harmless children. - One alas! is takenfrom me! would heaven but hear me for my poor Matilda! Father!intercede for her!"

"Every heart will bless her," cried Theodore with rapture.

"Be dumb, rash youth!" said Jerome. "And thou, fond Princess, contendnot with the Powers above! the Lord giveth, and the Lord taketh away:bless His holy name, and submit to his decrees."

"I do most devoutly," said Hippolita; "but will He not spare my onlycomfort? must Matilda perish too? - ah! Father, I came - but dismissthy son. No ear but thine must hear what I have to utter."

"May heaven grant thy every wish, most excellent Princess!" said Theodore retiring. Jerome frowned.

Hippolita then acquainted the Friar with the proposal she hadsuggested to Manfred, his approbation of it, and the tender of Matildathat he was gone to make to Frederic. Jerome could not conceal hisdislike of the notion, which he covered under pretence of theimprobability that Frederic, the nearest of blood to Alfonso, and whowas come to claim his succession, would yield to an alliance with theusurper of his right. But nothing could equal the perplexity of the Friar, when Hippolita confessed her readiness not to oppose theseparation, and demanded his opinion on the legality of heracquiescence. The Friar caught eagerly at her request of his advice,and without explaining his aversion to the proposed marriage of Manfred and Isabella, he painted to Hippolita in the most alarmingcolours the sinfulness of her consent, denounced judgments against herif she complied, and enjoined her in the severest terms to treat anysuch proposition with every mark of indignation and refusal.

Manfred, in the meantime, had broken his purpose to Frederic, andproposed the double marriage. That weak Prince, who had been struckwith the charms of Matilda, listened but too eagerly to the offer. Heforgot his enmity to Manfred, whom he saw but little hope ofdispossessing by force; and flattering himself that no issue mightsucceed from the union of his daughter with the tyrant, he looked uponhis own succession to the principality as facilitated by wedding Matilda. He made faint opposition to the proposal; affecting, forform only, not to acquiesce unless Hippolita should consent to thedivorce. Manfred took that upon himself.

Transported with his success, and impatient to see himself in asituation to expect sons, he hastened to his wife's apartment,determined to extort her compliance. He learned with indignation thatshe was absent at the convent. His guilt suggested to him that shehad probably been informed by Isabella of his purpose. He doubtedwhether her retirement to the convent did not import an intention ofremaining there, until she could raise obstacles to their divorce; andthe suspicions he had already entertained of Jerome, made himapprehend that the Friar would not only traverse his views, but mighthave inspired Hippolita with the resolution of talking sanctuary.

Impatient to unravel this clue, and to defeat its success, Manfredhastened to the convent, and arrived there as the Friar was earnestlyexhorting the Princess never to yield to the divorce.

"Madam," said Manfred, "what business drew you hither? why did you notawait my return from the Marquis?"

"I came to implore a blessing on your councils," replied Hippolita.

"My councils do not need a Friar's intervention," said Manfred; "andof all men living is that hoary traitor the only one whom you delightto confer with?"

"Profane Prince!" said Jerome; "is it at the altar that thou choosestto insult the servants of the altar? - but, Manfred, thy impiousschemes are known. Heaven and this virtuous lady know them - nay,frown not, Prince. The Church despises thy menaces. Her thunderswill be heard above thy wrath. Dare to proceed in thy cursed purposeof a divorce, until her sentence be known, and here I lance heranathema at thy head."

"Audacious rebel!" said Manfred, endeavouring to conceal the awe withwhich the Friar's words inspired him. "Dost thou presume to threatenthy lawful Prince?"

"Thou art no lawful Prince," said Jerome; "thou art no Prince—go,discuss thy claim with Frederic; and when that is done—"

"It is done," replied Manfred; "Frederic accepts Matilda's hand, andis content to waive his claim, unless I have no male issue"—as hespoke those words three drops of blood fell from the nose of Alfonso'sstatue. Manfred turned pale, and the Princess sank on her knees.

"Behold!" said the Friar; "mark this miraculous indication that theblood of Alfonso will never mix with that of Manfred!"

"My gracious Lord," said Hippolita, "let us submit ourselves toheaven. Think not thy ever obedient wife rebels against thyauthority. I have no will but that of my Lord and the Church. Tothat revered tribunal let us appeal. It does not depend on us toburst the bonds that unite us. If the Church shall approve thedissolution of our marriage, be it so - I have but few years, andthose of sorrow, to pass. Where can they be worn away so well as atthe foot of this altar, in prayers for thine and Matilda's safety?"

"But thou shalt not remain here until then," said Manfred. "Repairwith me to the castle, and there I will advise on the proper measuresfor a divorce; - but this meddling Friar comes not thither; myhospitable roof shall never more harbour a traitor - and for thy

Reverence's off-spring," continued he, "I banish him from mydominions. He, I ween, is no sacred personage, nor under theprotection of the Church. Whoever weds Isabella, it shall not be Father Falconara's started-up son."

"They start up," said the Friar, "who are suddenly beheld in the seatof lawful Princes; but they wither away like the grass, and theirplace knows them no more."

Manfred, casting a look of scorn at the Friar, led Hippolita forth;but at the door of the church whispered one of his attendants toremain concealed about the convent, and bring him instant notice, ifany one from the castle should repair thither.

CHAPTER - V

Every reflection which Manfred made on the Friar's behaviour,conspired to persuade him that Jerome was privy to an amour between Isabella and Theodore. But Jerome's new presumption, so dissonantfrom his former meekness, suggested still deeper apprehensions. The Prince even suspected that the Friar depended on some secret supportfrom Frederic, whose arrival, coinciding with the novel appearance of Theodore, seemed to bespeak a correspondence. Still more was hetroubled with the resemblance of Theodore to Alfonso's portrait. Thelatter he knew had unquestionably died without issue. Frederic hadconsented to bestow Isabella on him. These contradictions agitatedhis mind with numberless pangs.

He saw but two methods of extricating himself from his difficulties. The one was to resign his dominions to the Marquis—pride, ambition,and his reliance on ancient prophecies, which had pointed out apossibility of his preserving them to his posterity, combated thatthought. The other was to press his marriage with Isabella. Afterlong ruminating on these anxious thoughts, as he marched silently with Hippolita to the castle, he at last discoursed with that Princess onthe subject of his disquiet, and used every insinuating and plausibleargument to extract her consent to, even her promise of promoting thedivorce. Hippolita needed little persuasions to bend her to hispleasure. She endeavoured to win him over to the measure of resigninghis dominions; but finding her exhortations fruitless, she assuredhim, that as far as her conscience would allow, she would raise noopposition to a separation, though without better founded scruplesthan what he yet alleged, she would not engage to be active in demanding it.

This compliance, though inadequate, was sufficient to raise Manfred'shopes. He trusted that his power and wealth would easily advance hissuit at the court of Rome, whither he resolved to engage Frederic totake a journey on purpose. That Prince had discovered so much passionfor Matilda, that Manfred hoped to obtain all he wished by holding outor withdrawing his daughter's charms, according as the Marquis shouldappear more or less disposed to co-operate in his views. Even theabsence of Frederic would be a material point gained, until he couldtake further measures for his security.

Dismissing Hippolita to her apartment, he repaired to that of the Marquis; but crossing the great hall through which he was to pass hemet Bianca. The damsel he knew was in the confidence of both theyoung ladies. It immediately occurred to him to sift her on thesubject of Isabella and Theodore. Calling her aside into the recessof the oriel window of the hall, and soothing her with many fair wordsand promises, he demanded of her whether she knew aught of the stateof Isabella's affections.

"I! my Lord! no my Lord - yes my Lord - poor Lady! she is wonderfullyalarmed about her father's wounds; but I tell her he will do well;don't your Highness think so?"

"I do not ask you," replied Manfred, "what she thinks about herfather; but you are in her secrets. Come, be a good girl and tell me;is there any young man— ha!—you understand me."

"Lord bless me! understand your Highness? no, not I. I told her a fewvulnerary herbs and repose—"

"I am not talking," replied the Prince, impatiently, "about herfather; I know he will do well."

"Bless me, I rejoice to hear your Highness say so; for though Ithought it not right to let my young Lady despond, methought hisgreatness had a wan look, and a something—I remember when young Ferdinand was wounded by the Venetian—"

"Thou answerest from the point," interrupted Manfred; "but here, takethis jewel, perhaps that may fix thy attention - nay, no reverences;my favour shall not stop here—come, tell me truly; how stands Isabella's heart?"

"Well! your Highness has such a way!" said Bianca, "to be sure - butcan your Highness keep a secret? if it should ever come out of yourlips—"

"It shall not, it shall not," cried Manfred.

"Nay, but swear, your Highness."

"By my halidame, if it should ever be known that I said it - "

"Why, truth is truth, I do not think my Lady Isabella ever muchaffectioned my young Lord your son; yet he was a sweet youth as oneshould see; I am sure, if I had been a Princess - but bless me! Imust attend my Lady Matilda; she will marvel what is become of me."

"Stay," cried Manfred; "thou hast not satisfied my question. Hastthou ever carried any message, any letter?"

"I! good gracious!" cried Bianca; "I carry a letter? I would not tobe a Queen. I hope your Highness thinks, though I am poor, I amhonest. Did your Highness never hear what Count Marsigli offered me,when he came a wooing to my Lady Matilda?"

"I have not leisure," said Manfred, "to listen to thy tale. I do notquestion thy honesty. But it is thy duty to conceal nothing from me. How long has Isabella been acquainted with Theodore?"

"Nay, there is nothing can escape your Highness!" said Bianca; "notthat I know any thing of the matter. Theodore, to be sure, is aproper young man, and, as my Lady Matilda says, the very image of good Alfonso. Has not your Highness remarked it?"

"Yes, yes, - No - thou torturest me," said Manfred. "Where did theymeet? when?"

"Who! my Lady Matilda?" said Bianca.

"No, no, not Matilda: Isabella; when did Isabella first become acquainted with this Theodore!"

"Virgin Mary!" said Bianca, "how should I know?"

"Thou dost know," said Manfred; "and I must know; I will— "

"Lord! your Highness is not jealous of young Theodore!" said Bianca.

"Jealous! no, no. Why should I be jealous? perhaps I mean to unitethem - If I were sure Isabella would have no repugnance."

"Repugnance! no, I'll warrant her," said Bianca; "he is as comely ayouth as ever trod on Christian ground. We are all in love with him;there is not a soul in the castle but would be rejoiced to have himfor our Prince - I mean, when it shall please heaven to call your Highness to itself."

"Indeed!" said Manfred, "has it gone so far! oh! this cursed Friar! -but I must not lose time - go, Bianca, attend Isabella; but I chargethee, not a word of what has passed. Find out how she is affectedtowards Theodore; bring me good news, and that ring has a companion. Wait at the foot of the winding staircase: I am going to visit the Marquis, and will talk further with thee at my return."

Manfred, after some general conversation, desired Frederic to dismissthe two Knights, his companions, having to talk with him on urgentaffairs. As soon as they were alone, he began in artful guise to sound the Marquis on the subject of Matilda; and finding him disposed to hiswish, he let drop hints on the difficulties that would attend thecelebration of their marriage, unless - At that instant Bianca burstinto the room with a wildness in her look and gestures that spoke theutmost terror.

"Oh! my Lord, my Lord!" cried she; "we are all undone! it is comeagain! it is come again!"

"What is come again?" cried Manfred amazed.

"Oh! the hand! the Giant! the hand! - support me! I am terrified outof my senses," cried Bianca. "I will not sleep in the castle tonight. Where shall I go? my things may come after me to-morrow -would I had been content to wed Francesco! this comes of ambition!"

"What has terrified thee thus, young woman?" said the Marquis. "Thouart safe here; be not alarmed."

"Oh! your Greatness is wonderfully good," said Bianca, "but I dare not— no, pray let me go - I had rather leave everything behind me, thanstay another hour under this roof."

"Go to, thou hast lost thy senses," said Manfred. "Interrupt us not;we were communing on important matters - My Lord, this wench issubject to fits - Come with me, Bianca."

"Oh! the Saints! No," said Bianca, "for certain it comes to warn your Highness; why should it appear to me else? I say my prayers morningand evening - oh! if your Highness had believed Diego! 'Tis the samehand that he saw the foot to in the gallery-chamber - Father Jeromehas often told us the prophecy would be out one of these days - 'Bianca,' said he, 'mark my words—'"

"Thou ravest," said Manfred, in a rage; "be gone, and keep thesefooleries to frighten thy companions."

"What! my Lord," cried Bianca, "do you think I have seen nothing? goto the foot of the great stairs yourself - as I live I saw it."

"Saw what? tell us, fair maid, what thou hast seen," said Frederic.

"Can your Highness listen," said Manfred, "to the delirium of a sillywench, who has heard stories of apparitions until she believes them?"

"This is more than fancy," said the Marquis; "her terror is toonatural and too strongly impressed to be the work of imagination. Tell us, fair maiden, what it is has moved thee thus?"

"Yes, my Lord, thank your Greatness," said Bianca; "I believe I lookvery pale; I shall be better when I have recovered myself - I wasgoing to my Lady Isabella's chamber, by his Highness's order—"

"We do not want the circumstances," interrupted Manfred. "Since his Highness will have it so, proceed; but be brief."

"Lord! your Highness thwarts one so!" replied Bianca; "I fear my hair—I am sure I never in my life - well! as I was telling your Greatness, I was going by his Highness's order to my Lady Isabella'schamber; she lies in the watchet-coloured chamber, on the right hand,one pair of stairs: so when I came to the great stairs - I waslooking on his Highness's present here—"

"Grant me patience! " said Manfred, "will this wench never come to thepoint? what imports it to the Marquis, that I gave thee a bauble forthy faithful attendance on my daughter? we want to know what thou sawest."

"I was going to tell your Highness," said Bianca, "if you would permitme. So as I was rubbing the ring - I am sure I had not gone up threesteps, but I heard the rattling of armour; for all the world such aclatter as Diego says he heard when the Giant turned him about in the gallery—chamber."

"What Giant is this, my Lord?" said the Marquis; "is your castlehaunted by giants and goblins?"

"Lord! what, has not your Greatness heard the story of the Giant inthe gallery-chamber?" cried Bianca. "I marvel his Highness has nottold you; mayhap you do not know there is a prophecy—"

"This trifling is intolerable," interrupted Manfred. "Let us dismissthis silly wench, my Lord! we have more important affairs to discuss."

"By your favour," said Frederic, "these are no trifles. The enormoussabre I was directed to in the wood, yon casque, its fellow — are these visions of this poor maiden's brain?"

"So Jaquez thinks, may it please your Greatness," said Bianca. "Hesays this moon will not be out without our seeing some strangerevolution. For my part, I should not be surprised if it was tohappen to-morrow; for, as I was saying, when I heard the clattering ofarmour, I was all in a cold sweat. I looked up, and, if your Greatness will believe me, I saw upon the uppermost banister of thegreat stairs a hand in armour as big as big. I thought I should haveswooned. I never stopped until I came hither - would I were well outof this castle. My Lady Matilda told me but yester-morning that her Highness Hippolita knows something."

"Thou art an insolent!" cried Manfred. "Lord Marquis, it muchmisgives me that this scene is concerted to affront me. Are my owndomestics suborned to spread tales injurious to my honour? Pursueyour claim by manly daring; or let us bury our feuds, as was proposed,by the intermarriage of our children. But trust me, it ill becomes a Prince of your bearing to practise on mercenary wenches."

"I scorn your imputation," said Frederic. "Until this hour I neverset eyes on this damsel: I have given her no jewel. My Lord, my Lord, your conscience, your guilt accuses you, and would throw thesuspicion on me; but keep your daughter, and think no more of Isabella. The judgments already fallen on your house forbid mematching into it."

Manfred, alarmed at the resolute tone in which Frederic deliveredthese words, endeavoured to pacify him. Dismissing Bianca, he madesuch submissions to the Marquis, and threw in such artful encomiums on Matilda, that Frederic was once more staggered. However, as hispassion was of so recent a date, it could not at once surmount thescruples he had conceived. He had gathered enough from Bianca'sdiscourse to persuade him that heaven declared itself against Manfred. The proposed marriages too removed his claim to a distance; and theprincipality of Otranto was a stronger temptation than the contingentreversion of it with Matilda. Still he would not absolutely recedefrom his engagements; but purposing to gain time, he demanded of Manfred if it was true in fact that Hippolita consented to thedivorce. The Prince, transported to find no other obstacle, anddepending on his influence over his wife, assured the Marquis it wasso, and that he might satisfy himself of the truth from her own mouth.

As they were thus discoursing, word was brought that the banquet wasprepared. Manfred conducted Frederic to the great hall, where theywere received by Hippolita and the young Princesses. Manfred placedthe Marquis next to Matilda, and seated himself between his wife and Isabella. Hippolita comported herself with an easy gravity; but theyoung ladies were silent and melancholy. Manfred, who was determinedto pursue his point with the Marquis in the remainder of the evening,pushed on the feast until it waxed late; affecting unrestrainedgaiety, and plying Frederic with repeated goblets of wine. Thelatter, more upon his guard than Manfred wished, declined his frequentchallenges, on pretence of his late loss of blood; while the Prince,to raise his own disordered spirits, and to counterfeit unconcern,indulged himself in plentiful draughts, though not to the intoxicationof his senses.

The evening being far advanced, the banquet concluded. Manfred wouldhave withdrawn with Frederic; but the latter pleading weakness andwant of repose, retired to his chamber, gallantly telling the Princethat his daughter should amuse his Highness until himself could attendhim. Manfred accepted the party, and to the no small grief of Isabella, accompanied her to her apartment. Matilda waited on hermother to enjoy the freshness of the evening on the ramparts of the castle.

Soon as the company were dispersed their several ways, Frederic,quitting his chamber, inquired if Hippolita was alone, and was told byone of her attendants, who had not noticed her going forth, that atthat hour she generally withdrew to her oratory, where he probablywould find her. The Marquis, during the repast, had beheld Matildawith increase of passion. He now wished to find Hippolita in thedisposition her Lord had promised. The portents that had alarmed himwere forgotten in his desires. Stealing softly and unobserved to theapartment of Hippolita, he entered it with a resolution to encourageher acquiescence to the divorce, having perceived that Manfred wasresolved to make the possession of Isabella an unalterable condition,before he would grant Matilda to his wishes.

The Marquis was not surprised at the silence that reigned in the Princess's apartment. Concluding her, as he had been advertised, inher oratory, he passed on. The door was ajar; the evening gloomy andovercast. Pushing open the door gently, he saw a person kneelingbefore the altar. As he approached nearer, it seemed not a woman, butone in a long woollen weed, whose back was towards him. The personseemed absorbed in prayer. The Marquis was about to return, when thefigure, rising, stood some moments fixed in meditation, withoutregarding him. The Marquis, expecting the holy person to come forth,and meaning to excuse his uncivil interruption, said,

"Reverend Father, I sought the Lady Hippolita."

"Hippolita!" replied a hollow voice; "camest thou to this castle toseek Hippolita?" and then the figure, turning slowly round, discoveredto Frederic the fleshless jaws and empty sockets of a skeleton, wraptin a hermit's cowl.

"Angels of grace protect me!" cried Frederic, recoiling.

"Deserve their protection!" said the Spectre. Frederic, falling onhis knees, adjured the phantom to take pity on him.

"Dost thou not remember me?" said the apparition. "Remember the woodof Joppa!"

"Art thou that holy hermit?" cried Frederic, trembling. "Can I doaught for thy eternal peace?"

"Wast thou delivered from bondage," said the spectre, "to pursuecarnal delights? Hast thou forgotten the buried sabre, and the behestof Heaven engraven on it?"

"I have not, I have not," said Frederic; "but say, blest spirit, whatis thy errand to me? What remains to be done?"

"To forget Matilda!" said the apparition; and vanished.

Frederic's blood froze in his veins. For some minutes he remainedmotionless. Then falling prostrate on his face before the altar, hebesought the intercession of every saint for pardon. A flood of tearssucceeded to this transport; and the image of the beauteous Matildarushing in spite of him on his thoughts, he lay on the ground in aconflict of penitence and passion. Ere he could recover from thisagony of his spirits, the Princess Hippolita with a taper in her handentered the oratory alone. Seeing a man without motion on the floor,she gave a shriek, concluding him dead. Her fright brought Fredericto himself. Rising suddenly, his face bedewed with tears, he wouldhave rushed from her presence; but Hippolita stopping him, conjuredhim in the most plaintive accents to explain the cause of hisdisorder, and by what strange chance she had found him there in that posture.

"Ah, virtuous Princess!" said the Marquis, penetrated with grief, and stopped.

"For the love of Heaven, my Lord," said Hippolita, "disclose the causeof this transport! What mean these doleful sounds, this alarmingexclamation on my name? What woes has heaven still in store for thewretched Hippolita? Yet silent! By every pitying angel, I adjurethee, noble Prince," continued she, falling at his feet, "to disclosethe purport of what lies at thy heart. I see thou feelest for me;thou feelest the sharp pangs that thou inflictest—speak, for pity! Does aught thou knowest concern my child?"

"I cannot speak," cried Frederic, bursting from her. "Oh, Matilda!"

Quitting the Princess thus abruptly, he hastened to his own apartment. At the door of it he was accosted by Manfred, who flushed by wine andlove had come to seek him, and to propose to waste some hours of thenight in music and revelling. Frederic, offended at an invitation sodissonant from the mood of his soul, pushed him rudely aside, andentering his chamber, flung the door intemperately against Manfred,and bolted it inwards. The haughty Prince, enraged at thisunaccountable behaviour, withdrew in a frame of mind capable of themost fatal excesses. As he crossed the court, he was met by thedomestic whom he had planted at the convent as a spy on Jerome and Theodore. This man, almost breathless with the haste he had made,informed his Lord that Theodore, and some lady from the castle were,at that instant, in private conference at the tomb of Alfonso in St. Nicholas's church. He had dogged Theodore thither, but the gloominessof the night had prevented his discovering who the woman was.

Manfred, whose spirits were inflamed, and whom Isabella had drivenfrom her on his urging his passion with too little reserve, did notdoubt but the inquietude she had expressed had been occasioned by herimpatience to meet Theodore. Provoked by this conjecture, and enragedat her father, he hastened secretly to the great church. Glidingsoftly between the aisles, and guided by an imperfect gleam ofmoonshine that shone faintly through the illuminated windows, he stoletowards the tomb of Alfonso, to which he was directed by indistinctwhispers of the persons he sought. The first sounds he coulddistinguish were—

"Does it, alas! depend on me? Manfred will never permit our union."

"No, this shall prevent it!" cried the tyrant, drawing his dagger, andplunging it over her shoulder into the bosom of the person that spoke.

"Ah, me, I am slain!" cried Matilda, sinking. "Good heaven, receivemy soul!"

"Savage, inhuman monster, what hast thou done!" cried Theodore,rushing on him, and wrenching his dagger from him.

"Stop, stop thy impious hand!" cried Matilda; "it is my father!"

Manfred, waking as from a trance, beat his breast, twisted his handsin his locks, and endeavoured to recover his dagger from Theodore todespatch himself. Theodore, scarce less distracted, and onlymastering the transports of his grief to assist Matilda, had now byhis cries drawn some of the monks to his aid. While part of themendeavoured, in concert with the afflicted Theodore, to stop the bloodof the dying Princess, the rest prevented Manfred from laying violenthands on himself.

Matilda, resigning herself patiently to her fate, acknowledged withlooks of grateful love the zeal of Theodore. Yet oft as her faintnesswould permit her speech its way, she begged the assistants to comforther father. Jerome, by this time, had learnt the fatal news, andreached the church. His looks seemed to reproach Theodore, butturning to Manfred, he said,

"Now, tyrant! behold the completion of woe fulfilled on thy impiousand devoted head! The blood of Alfonso cried to heaven for vengeance;and heaven has permitted its altar to be polluted by assassination,that thou mightest shed thy own blood at the foot of that Prince's sepulchre!"

"Cruel man!" cried Matilda, "to aggravate the woes of a parent; mayheaven bless my father, and forgive him as I do! My Lord, my gracious

Sire, dost thou forgive thy child? Indeed, I came not hither to meet

Theodore. I found him praying at this tomb, whither my mother sent meto intercede for thee, for her - dearest father, bless your child, andsay you forgive her."

"Forgive thee! Murderous monster!" cried Manfred, "can assassinsforgive? I took thee for Isabella; but heaven directed my bloody handto the heart of my child. Oh, Matilda! - I cannot utter it - canstthou forgive the blindness of my rage?"

"I can, I do; and may heaven confirm it!" said Matilda; "but while Ihave life to ask it - oh! my mother! what will she feel? Will youcomfort her, my Lord? Will you not put her away? Indeed she lovesyou! Oh, I am faint! bear me to the castle. Can I live to have herclose my eyes?"

Theodore and the monks besought her earnestly to suffer herself to beborne into the convent; but her instances were so pressing to becarried to the castle, that placing her on a litter, they conveyed herthither as she requested. Theodore, supporting her head with his arm,and hanging over her in an agony of despairing love, still endeavouredto inspire her with hopes of life. Jerome, on the other side,comforted her with discourses of heaven, and holding a crucifix beforeher, which she bathed with innocent tears, prepared her for herpassage to immortality. Manfred, plunged in the deepest affliction,followed the litter in despair.

Ere they reached the castle, Hippolita, informed of the dreadfulcatastrophe, had flown to meet her murdered child; but when she sawthe afflicted procession, the mightiness of her grief deprived her ofher senses, and she fell lifeless to the earth in a swoon. Isabellaand Frederic, who attended her, were overwhelmed in almost equalsorrow. Matilda alone seemed insensible to her own situation: everythought was lost in tenderness for her mother.

Ordering the litter to stop, as soon as Hippolita was brought toherself, she asked for her father. He approached, unable to speak. Matilda, seizing his hand and her mother's, locked them in her own,and then clasped them to her heart. Manfred could not support thisact of pathetic piety. He dashed himself on the ground, and cursedthe day he was born. Isabella, apprehensive that these struggles ofpassion were more than Matilda could support, took upon herself toorder Manfred to be borne to his apartment, while she caused Matildato be conveyed to the nearest chamber. Hippolita, scarce more alivethan her daughter, was regardless of everything but her; but when thetender Isabella's care would have likewise removed her, while thesurgeons examined Matilda's wound, she cried,

"Remove me! never, never! I lived but in her, and will expire with her."

Matilda raised her eyes at her mother's voice, but closed them againwithout speaking. Her sinking pulse and the damp coldness of her handsoon dispelled all hopes of recovery. Theodore followed the surgeonsinto the outer chamber, and heard them pronounce the fatal sentencewith a transport equal to frenzy.

"Since she cannot live mine," cried he, "at least she shall be mine indeath! Father! Jerome! will you not join our hands?" cried he to the Friar, who, with the Marquis, had accompanied the surgeons.

"What means thy distracted rashness?" said Jerome. "Is this an hourfor marriage?"

"It is, it is," cried Theodore. "Alas! there is no other!"

"Young man, thou art too unadvised," said Frederic. "Dost thou thinkwe are to listen to thy fond transports in this hour of fate? What pretensions hast thou to the Princess?"

"Those of a Prince," said Theodore; "of the sovereign of Otranto. This reverend man, my father, has informed me who I am."

"Thou ravest," said the Marquis. "There is no Prince of Otranto butmyself, now Manfred, by murder, by sacrilegious murder, has forfeitedall pretensions."

"My Lord," said Jerome, assuming an air of command, "he tells youtrue. It was not my purpose the secret should have been divulged sosoon, but fate presses onward to its work. What his hot-headedpassion has revealed, my tongue confirms. Know, Prince, that when Alfonso set sail for the Holy Land—"

"Is this a season for explanations?" cried Theodore. "Father, comeand unite me to the Princess; she shall be mine! In every other thing I will dutifully obey you. My life! my adored Matilda!" continued Theodore, rushing back into the inner chamber, "will you not be mine? Will you not bless your—"

Isabella made signs to him to be silent, apprehending the Princess wasnear her end.

"What, is she dead?" cried Theodore; "is it possible!"

The violence of his exclamations brought Matilda to herself. Liftingup her eyes, she looked round for her mother.

"Life of my soul, I am here!" cried Hippolita; "think not I will quit thee!"

"Oh! you are too good," said Matilda. "But weep not for me, mymother! I am going where sorrow never dwells - Isabella, thou hastloved me; wouldst thou not supply my fondness to this dear, dearwoman? Indeed I am faint!"

"Oh! my child! my child!" said Hippolita in a flood of tears, "can Inot withhold thee a moment?"

"It will not be," said Matilda; "commend me to heaven - Where is myfather? forgive him, dearest mother - forgive him my death; it was anerror. Oh! I had forgotten - dearest mother, I vowed never to see Theodore more - perhaps that has drawn down this calamity - but it wasnot intentional - can you pardon me?"

"Oh! wound not my agonising soul!" said Hippolita; "thou never couldstoffend me —Alas! she faints! help! help!"

"I would say something more," said Matilda, struggling, "but it cannotbe - Isabella - Theodore - for my sake—Oh!—" she expired.

Isabella and her women tore Hippolita from the corse; but Theodorethreatened destruction to all who attempted to remove him from it. Heprinted a thousand kisses on her clay-cold hands, and uttered everyexpression that despairing love could dictate.

Isabella, in the meantime, was accompanying the afflicted Hippolita toher apartment; but, in the middle of the court, they were met by Manfred, who, distracted with his own thoughts, and anxious once moreto behold his daughter, was advancing to the chamber where she lay. As the moon was now at its height, he read in the countenances of thisunhappy company the event he dreaded.

"What! is she dead?" cried he in wild confusion. A clap of thunder atthat instant shook the castle to its foundations; the earth rocked,and the clank of more than mortal armour was heard behind. Fredericand Jerome thought the last day was at hand. The latter, forcing Theodore along with them, rushed into the court. The moment Theodoreappeared, the walls of the castle behind Manfred were thrown down witha mighty force, and the form of Alfonso, dilated to an immensemagnitude, appeared in the centre of the ruins.

"Behold in Theodore the true heir of Alfonso!" said the vision: Andhaving pronounced those words, accompanied by a clap of thunder, itascended solemnly towards heaven, where the clouds parting asunder,the form of St. Nicholas was seen, and receiving Alfonso's shade, theywere soon wrapt from mortal eyes in a blaze of glory.

The beholders fell prostrate on their faces, acknowledging the divinewill. The first that broke silence was Hippolita.

"My Lord," said she to the desponding Manfred, "behold the vanity ofhuman greatness! Conrad is gone! Matilda is no more! In Theodore weview the true Prince of Otranto. By what miracle he is so I know not—suffice it to us, our doom is pronounced! shall we not, can we butdedicate the few deplorable hours we have to live, in deprecating thefurther wrath of heaven? heaven ejects us—whither can we fly, but toyon holy cells that yet offer us a retreat."

"Thou guiltless but unhappy woman! unhappy by my crimes!" replied Manfred, "my heart at last is open to thy devout admonitions. Oh!could - but it cannot be—ye are lost in wonder—let me at last dojustice on myself! To heap shame on my own head is all thesatisfaction I have left to offer to offended heaven. My story hasdrawn down these judgments: Let my confession atone—but, ah! whatcan atone for usurpation and a murdered child? a child murdered in aconsecrated place? List, sirs, and may this bloody record be awarning to future tyrants!"

"Alfonso, ye all know, died in the Holy Land—ye would interrupt me;ye would say he came not fairly to his end—it is most true—whyelse this bitter cup which Manfred must drink to the dregs. Ricardo,my grandfather, was his chamberlain—I would draw a veil over myancestor's crimes—but it is in vain! Alfonso died by poison. Afictitious will declared Ricardo his heir. His crimes pursued him -yet he lost no Conrad, no Matilda! I pay the price of usurpation forall! A storm overtook him. Haunted by his guilt he vowed to St. Nicholas to found a church and two convents, if he lived to reach Otranto. The sacrifice was accepted: the saint appeared to him in adream, and promised that Ricardo's posterity should reign in Otrantountil the rightful owner should be grown too large to inhabit thecastle, and as long as issue male from Ricardo's loins should remainto enjoy it— alas! alas! nor male nor female, except myself, remainsof all his wretched race! I have done—the woes of these three daysspeak the rest. How this young man can be Alfonso's heir I know not -yet I do not doubt it. His are these dominions; I resign them - yet Iknew not Alfonso had an heir - I question not the will of heaven -poverty and prayer must fill up the woeful space, until Manfred shallbe summoned to Ricardo."

"What remains is my part to declare," said Jerome. "When Alfonso setsail for the Holy Land he was driven by a storm to the coast of Sicily. The other vessel, which bore Ricardo and his train, as your Lordship must have heard, was separated from him."

"It is most true," said Manfred; "and the title you give me is morethan an outcast can claim —well! be it so—proceed."

Jerome blushed, and continued. "For three months Lord Alfonso waswind-bound in Sicily. There he became enamoured of a fair virginnamed Victoria. He was too pious to tempt her to forbidden pleasures. They were married. Yet deeming this amour incongruous with the holyvow of arms by which he was bound, he determined to conceal theirnuptials until his return from the Crusade, when he purposed to seekand acknowledge her for his lawful wife. He left her pregnant.

During his absence she was delivered of a daughter. But scarce hadshe felt a mother's pangs ere she heard the fatal rumour of her Lord'sdeath, and the succession of Ricardo. What could a friendless,helpless woman do? Would her testimony avail?—yet, my lord, I havean authentic writing —"

"It needs not," said Manfred; "the horrors of these days, the visionwe have but now seen, all corroborate thy evidence beyond a thousandparchments. Matilda's death and my expulsion — "

"Be composed, my Lord," said Hippolita; "this holy man did not mean torecall your griefs." Jerome proceeded.

"I shall not dwell on what is needless. The daughter of which Victoria was delivered, was at her maturity bestowed in marriage onme. Victoria died; and the secret remained locked in my breast. Theodore's narrative has told the rest."

The Friar ceased. The disconsolate company retired to the remainingpart of the castle. In the morning Manfred signed his abdication ofthe principality, with the approbation of Hippolita, and each took onthem the habit of religion in the neighbouring convents. Fredericoffered his daughter to the new Prince, which Hippolita's tendernessfor Isabella concurred to promote. But Theodore's grief was too freshto admit the thought of another love; and it was not until afterfrequent discourses with Isabella of his dear Matilda, that he waspersuaded he could know no happiness but in the society of one withwhom he could for ever indulge the melancholy that had takenpossession of his soul.